LOVE MATCH

Praise For Love Match

"Let's see…funny, romantic, to-die-for hero, yep, Megan Hart's *Love Match* has everything needed for the perfect romance. I couldn't put *Love Match* down. Don't walk, run to read *Love Match* today!"

Karen Troxel
Author of *Web Story*

"*Love Match* had me laughing out loud as I was reading it. This story is one mishap after another. My favorite scene was when Hal was 'fixing' the radiator and ended up giving Lili a black eye. This story isn't all humor though, as both Lili and Hal have to come to terms with the relationships in their respective pasts. The story moves quickly and never bogs down. The characters are all well written and easily identified with. This is truly a wonderful story and I cannot recommend it highly enough."

—Chere Gruver,
Member of RIO
(Reviewers International Organization)

ALSO BY MEGAN HART

LOVE MATCH

BY

MEGAN HART

AMBER QUILL PRESS, LLC

http://www.amberquill.com

LOVE MATCH
AN AMBER QUILL PRESS BOOK

This book is a work of fiction. All names, characters,
locations, and incidents are products of the author's imagination,
or have been used fictitiously. Any resemblance to actual persons
living or dead, locales, or events is entirely coincidental.

Amber Quill Press, LLC
http://www.amberquill.com

Layout and Formatting provided by: ElementalAlchemy.com

PUBLISHED IN THE UNITED STATES OF AMERICA

To my own Eagle Scout, David, who's always prepared

CHAPTER 1

"Are you sure that's the one you want, dear?" Ms. Whitehead held out the heavy binder and frowned over her chic, gold-rimmed glasses at Lili Alster. "I have to say, he's not one of our more popular models."

Ms. Whitehead flipped a few pages toward the front of the thick sheaf of plastic-covered photographs, then pointed to the picture of a man with blond, shoulder-length hair. His limpid eyes, chiseled jaw and bronzed skin, coupled with the hair and the muscular body, strongly reminded Lili of a romance novel cover model.

"No, thanks. He's not quite me."

Ms. Whitehead laughed. "Honey, are you sure? Rick is mostly anybody. Take another look."

Lili smiled politely, but opened the binder back to the page she'd first indicated. "My family would never believe me if I showed up with a man like that on my arm. No, I think—" She paused to read the name on the photograph. "Harold. I think he'll be perfect for my needs."

Ms. Whitehead sighed and slid the binder back over her desk, then heaved it onto a bookshelf laden with similar books. "All right, honey, if you say so. Hal doesn't get much work, poor thing."

"Why?" Lili asked wryly. "Because he wears glasses and has short hair? Because he looks like a normal guy and not a muscle bound god of love?"

"Er—well." Ms. Whitehead paused then patted her silver bouffant with one bejeweled hand. "Ahem. I'd say that's one reason."

Misgiving fluttered in Lili's already churning stomach. "And the others?"

"Hal means well, Miss Alster. He means very well, in fact. He's one of the more enthusiastic models here at LoveMatch. But he doesn't get much repeat business, I have to be honest with you."

Lili swallowed hard, waiting for the bad news. He was a drug addict. He liked to rough up his customers. He had chronic halitosis. What could be so dire that Ms. Whitehead, the LoveMatch goddess herself, could barely bring herself to reveal it?"

"Hal's a bit clumsy," Ms. Whitehead said finally with a glance over her glasses that told Lili she wasn't exaggerating. "And his social skills are a little less developed than we usually prefer in our men. But he's enrolled in all our courses and is improving quite nicely. I only warn you because you told me how important it was for you to have date for this family party."

Not just a date, Lili thought. *A fiancé.* "Social skills. You mean like holding the door open for me and pulling out my chair? Stuff like that? Because that doesn't really matter. In fact, the less of that, the better."

Ms. Whitehead looked uncomfortable. She tapped her long, crimson, lacquered nails lightly on top of her desk. At last she pulled open one of her file drawers and took out a thin folder. Opening it, she removed a sheet of paper, filled in a few blanks, and pushed it across the desk to Lili.

"Since you seem to have your heart set on Hal," Ms. Whitehead said, "I'll tell you what I'm going to do for you, honey. I'm going to give you a free night out with him, compliments of LoveMatch. You can see for yourself if he is the right man to escort you to your family shindig. If it doesn't work out, you can come back and choose one of our other models. Okay?"

A free night out sounded all right. Lili looked over the paper, which turned out to be a standard release form. She'd read the one included with her information packet already, and so now she signed the bottom with the pen Ms. Whitehead held out. The white-haired woman then tucked the paper back in the folder, twirled her desk chair toward another set of filing cabinets, and pulled out another file.

"Here's some background information on Hal," she said, pushing a sheet of paper over the desk.

There wasn't much written on it. "Favorite music, "Weird" Al Yankovic?" Lili smiled. She liked "Weird" Al, too, but she wasn't sure she'd have listed him as her favorite. "Hobbies are reading, bike riding, and going for long, romantic walks along the beach in the moonlight."

Except for the last, which was so obviously added to spice up his file it was almost laughable, he didn't sound bad so far. She quickly read further. He'd gone to college, mastered in accounting. So he was good at math. He'd also marked he was currently attending school, but not what for.

"I'm sure he'll be fine," she said. "What's the next step?"

"For the initial date, I can make the arrangements for you. You pick the place and time, and I'll contact your escort to make sure he's available." Ms. Whitehead ran her finger down the lines in the appointment book. "He usually is. As I said, LoveMatch will pick up the escort fee, and this time, dinner is on us. But after that—"

"Of course," Lili said. She paged through her day planner, though she knew her evenings were free. Like Hal, she was usually available. "Wednesday night looks good for me. MJ's Coffeehouse at the Allen Theater in Annville?"

Ms. Whitehead nodded. "We can have Hal pick you up at home, or if you prefer, you can meet him at the date location. Most of our clients choose to meet their escorts in a public place first—although a good many of them end up letting their dates escort them home."

Lili ignored the older woman's wink. She wasn't hiring Hal to be her sex toy. She needed him to act as her fiancé for one week, during her grandparents' sixtieth anniversary celebration. She needed him to treat her terribly, act like a total jerk in front of her family, and break things off with her in such a way they'd never ask about him again.

"If I do decide that Hal will work out, can I be sure he's available for the entire week?"

"Many of our clients have taken their escorts on vacations with them. Most of our men make a very nice living doing what they do. I shouldn't imagine there'll be any problem."

Not for an all-expense paid vacation and a nice fat fee, too. Lili cringed at what this was going to do to her bank account, but getting her family's attention away from her love life was worth any price. Ian's insurance money would have paid for a nice exotic vacation or a big screen television. Instead it would pay for a new fiancé.

"Fine." Lili shook Ms. Whitehead's hand. "Seven-thirty?"

"Wonderful." Ms. Whitehead's lips, crimson to match her nails, spread into a genuine smile. "Good luck, dear."

"Thank you," Lili said. She'd need it.

* * *

The smell of sweat was overpowering. Hal Kessler swallowed

3

heavily and kept his feet moving on the elliptical trainer. Twenty minutes to go and he'd be done.

"So's I was saying," Rick Mallard went on, oblivious to Hal's silence. "The chick really dug me, you know? And she was stacked! And loaded, too. So her face was could crack a mirror, hey, so what? She took me to Visaggio's for dinner three times in one week."

"Huh," Hal said.

"So's of course I had to make sure I gave her dessert," Rick said with a leer.

The tan blond man adjusted the buttons on his trainer, stepping up the pace. Even though his feet were going twice as fast as Hal's, Rick didn't even sound out of breath. His back muscles, clearly visible through the white mesh tank shirt he wore, pumped and worked as he strode. Hal could work out for years and his back would never look like that.

"Huh," Hal said again, noncommittally. It was about all he could manage without puffing embarrassingly.

"Then this other broad, name's Marsha, hips like a battleship, know what I mean? But she's loaded, too. She took me to Neiman Marcus and bought me a tux just so's we could go to the theater."

"A client bought me a book of poetry once," Hal offered. He tried not to let a gasp punctuate every word.

Rick shot him a look. "Wow, Kessler. That's uh—cool."

It had been very cool, Hal thought. *Soloman's Song of Songs.* Love poetry, filled with rich and passionate imagery. Mary Kate Peterson had been that client's name, and one of the few who'd hired him more than once. She'd never asked him for any "dessert," though.

"So's, anyway—" The rapid beeping of a pager interrupted Rick's story.

Rick's hand went automatically to the small, black box clipped at his waistband, and he pressed the button. The beeping continued. It took Rick's look of comical surprise to make Hal realize it wasn't Rick's pager making the noise.It was his own.

"Kessler, it's you." Rick shook his head and tossed his long, blond hair over his shoulders. "Go for it, dude."

Hal fumbled with the pager's tiny buttons. The beeping stopped abruptly, but because he'd had to let go of the elliptical machine's handrail, Hal lost his balance. Suddenly the machine was going too fast for his feet, and he couldn't keep up. As he tried to stop the machine and get off all at the same time the elastic cuff on his sweatpants got caught on the edge of the pedal. The still-moving pedals threw him forward, into the trainer's control panel, and he banged his head on the handrail. Hal dropped his pager.

It seemed that every eye in the entire gym was on him as he extricated himself from the damnable machine and bent to pick up his pager. Probably because everyone was staring at him. Hal kept his head high, even as he tripped over his own towel and knocked against Rick's machine.

He didn't imagine the sniggers and muffled chortles following him as he made his way to the locker room. His face burned, and he ducked, with relief, through the quiet doorway. He'd suffered humiliations before at this gym, but never one on such a grand scale.

The pager beeped again, more insistently this time, as he fumbled with his locker. Guys like Rick got paged so often that answering a beep was second nature to them. Guys like Rick, who had barely two brain cells to rub together, managed to exercise, answer their calls and look great doing it. Hal had advanced business and accounting degrees, and yet he could barely walk and chew gum at the same time. He sighed in despair as his fingers hit the wrong numbers on the phone and he had to redial. Why was he such a huge klutz?

"You've got a date for Wednesday night, honey," Muriel Whitehead told him without preamble. "Seven-thirty, MJ's Coffeehouse in Annville. Casual dress."

"Thanks, Muriel."

He heard her flipping through her appointment book. "This could be a big job, kiddo. A week in the Poconos."

Her unspoken advice, *Don't screw this up,* vibrated through the phone's tiny earpiece. She knew as well as he did how much he needed this job. Better, actually, since he still had outstanding debt for some of the LoveMatch training classes he'd taken.

"Client's name?" Hal managed to dig through his gym bag and find his notepad and a pen. It even had ink in it.

She told him, along with the physical description and some background information. "She's not exactly looking for Romeo, Hal."

He could have guessed that. "I'll be there."

"Hal?"

"What time is it?"

"It's—" Hal checked his wrist and realized his watch was missing. There was no clock in the locker room either.

"Never mind, honey." Muriel's sigh was huge, even through the tiny speaker. "You're at the gym? Check your bag."

It was right there. "My watch says 11:30."

Another sigh. "Honey, it's 12:17."

Punctuality was one of LoveMatch's requirements in its employees. "Thanks, Muriel."

"Hal, did you ever think that this might not be the career for you?"

He had thought that, many times, but always some job came through and the resulting paycheck made it all worthwhile. "I need the money."

"I know you do, sweetheart." Muriel made kissy noises into the phone. "Don't forget, and don't be late. And for Heaven's sake, make sure your socks match!"

"I'm not a complete schlub," Hal complained, though reflexively he'd noted her suggestion in the margin of his notepad. *Check socks.*

"You're a sweet boy," Muriel said, as though that would make him feel better. "And, Hal, this one's a freebie."

He groaned. "Muriel—"

She tutted into the phone. "No complaints! After what happened the last time—"

"All right." She didn't have to say any more. Hal's last date had been a true comedy of errors without the comedy. He was lucky the client hadn't sought legal action instead of demanding a refund.

Muriel said goodbye, and Hal clicked off the phone. He looked at the name he'd written down. Lili Alster. It was a pretty name, but he had no illusions about the face that went with it. Gorgeous women, as a rule, just didn't contact LoveMatch, and most women who did use the service chose guys who looked like Rick.

Hal took a minute to adjust his watch to the proper time, realizing as he did so that he was going to be late for his Healing Touch class. He let out a strangled curse. *Could the day get any worse?* Shoving his stuff into gym bag, he left the gym without bothering to shower. He couldn't be late for class. Again.

The gym door opened out into a side alley right next to the LoveMatch offices. Narrow and dim on the best days, today the small street was even more difficult to navigate because of the construction going on at the far end. Grateful he hadn't taken off his sneakers, Hal slung his bag over his shoulder and set off at a sprint down the debris-littered concrete. If he ran fast enough he'd be able to get to class on time—

All at once, Hal's feet were moving, but the rest of him was not. As the ground came up to meet him, he had only one thought. *I'm not going to make it class today.*

*   *   *

The man sitting in front of her with the bleeding nose and swollen cheek looked so forlorn, Lili couldn't help feeling sorry for him. Also, annoyed. Because of him, she was going to be late getting back from lunch. The collision had also put a runner in her last pair of taupe tights, scuffed her brand new shoes and left her knee scraped and bleeding.

"I'm so sorry," he moaned over and over again. He took the twisted tissues out of his left nostril, but immediately stuck them back in when the blood began flowing again. "I'm really sorry."

"It's all right," Lili said. What was one supposed to do in situations like this anyway? She felt bad just leaving the guy sitting on the curb, but she really was late. "We both should've been more careful."

"You don't understand," said the man morosely. His voice, perhaps because of the tissues in his nose, was deep and throaty. He held up a pair of glasses, the frames twisted from the collision, then tossed them down. "Stuff like this happens to me all the time. I'm a walking disaster."

"I'm sure it's not that bad," Lili said absently, already checking her watch. "It could've happened to anyone."

"Is your knee all right? I'll pay for your dry cleaning, if you want."

Of her ruined tights? Of her knee? The rest of her was fine, except for the shoes, which needed a good polishing. "No, that's okay. Really. Listen, I have to run—"

"Sure, sure," said the man letting his head droop. "I'm so sorry."

"Really, don't worry about it," Lili said sympathetically. Under other circumstances she'd be livid, but this guy was just so pathetic she couldn't find it in herself to stay mad. "No harm done."

To her alarm, the man's head kept drooping and drooping. Instead of staying upright in his seat at the curb, he fell forward. Crunch. Right onto the sidewalk.

With a shriek, Lili rolled him over. His face had gone a sickly shade of greenish white and his eyes were fluttering.

"Blood," he muttered in a garbled tone. "Can't. Stand. Blood!"

Lili reached into her shoulder bag and pulled out her water bottle. Popping the screwtop, she squirted the entire contents of the nearly full bottle right in the man's face. With a choking gasp, he sat straight up, water streaming down his cheeks. The tissue in his nose disintegrated, sending a fresh stream of blood to paint his upper lip. His cheeks were pink, though, instead of the ghastly green, and he didn't look like he was going to faint again.

"I'm sorry!" he cried.

"Shut up," Lili said smartly. "Here."

She reached again into her voluminous bag and pulled out a travel package of baby wipes. Having a dozen nieces and nephews had taught her the importance of always carrying wipes. She gave them to the poor soul in front of her.

"Thank you," said the man quietly. "I can't tell you how embarrassed I am."

"You are a real mess," Lili said sympathetically, watching him.

Cleaned up, he wasn't bad looking, even with the ridiculous remains of the twist of tissue in his nose. His thick, wheat-colored hair would benefit from a more stylish cut, but he had strong, large features, including a wide mouth that might look nice with a smile on it. She could see that his eyes, now they weren't rolling back in his head, were light. Blue...or maybe green. He was almost, but not quite handsome, and he looked somehow familiar.

"Do I know you?" she asked.

"I sure hope not," the man replied.

Impulsively, she held out her hand. He took it in his own, engulfing her fingers with his own much larger ones. His handshake was firm, if a little damp from the wipes. He stood, and she saw that he was very tall. She had to tilt her head just to meet his eyes.

"I'm—" she began, but the wailing siren and flashing lights of a police car cut off her introduction.

The car skidded to a stop just beyond the construction site, and two uniformed officers leapt out. To Lili's shock, each held a gun, aimed right at them.

*   *   *

If Hal hadn't been staring so hard at the lovely face of the woman he'd knocked over, he might have seen the cop car sooner. As it was, until the police officers shouted at him to put his hands up and step away from the woman, he'd just been lost in her lovely eyes. Mesmerized, he followed the movement of her hand as it brushed her dark, shoulder-length hair away from her face.

"Move it, buddy!" The first cop, a tall, graying man with a football player's build, stepped forward and motioned with his gun.

Maybe it was the knock on the head, but Hal couldn't figure out why they were shouting at him. The second, much younger officer, got even more aggressive.

"Move away from the woman! Now!"

The woman shifted her deep brown eyes away from Hal's to stare at the officers. "I think they mean you."

Hal turned, hands up. "This must be a misunderstanding—"

"Are you all right, ma'am?" The older cop crossed to them, looking Hal over warily before putting his gun away. "We got a report of an attack in progress here. A witness in the office building over there said she saw this man knock you down and assault you. She thought he might be drunk."

If only the ground would open and swallow him up. Hal had been humiliated so many times in his life he thought he'd gotten used to it by now, but this was worse than anything he'd ever been through. The dried crust of blood itched on his upper lip, and both his knees and palms throbbed with scrapes from when he'd hit the pavement. He wouldn't blame the woman for having him hauled away in handcuffs.

Instead, she just smiled and shook her head. "It was completely an accident, officer. No harm, no foul."

Her sports terminology seemed to put the officer at ease. The younger of the two policemen seemed disappointed to be putting away his weapon. Hal was relieved.

"Are you sure, ma'am?" The older cop looked Hal up and down with a bemused expression. "Then again, he does look worse off than you. Maybe the witness saw you attacking him."

They all laughed heartily at that, even Hal. His chuckle came out through gritted teeth. The woman quickly explained the collision. She nicely omitted the part where Hal almost passed out at the sight of his own blood.

"If you're sure you're all right," the older cop said with a tilt of his head toward the woman.

"Fine, fine," she assured them. She checked her watch, a gesture Hal had seen her make several times over the past few minutes.

Time! What time is it? His gaze flew to his own wrist, but the fall had shattered his cheap watch's face. Whatever time it was, he was sure he was late.

The policemen had already gone back to their car and driven away, leaving Hal and the woman to stand awkwardly on the sidewalk. She gave him a weird, little smile, and Hal realized he was staring.

"I'm—"

The woman said pleasantly, "Like I said, no harm done. Now, if you'll excuse me, I've really got to run."

She checked her watch and a shadow of annoyance passed over her face. She muttered something under her breath that sounded like "Late again," while shaking her head. She tucked her water bottle and the baby wipes back in her purse. With a little wave at Hal, she set off down the alley again with a purposeful stride.

"Hope the rest of your day goes a lot better," she called over her shoulder.

"Thanks," Hal said. "It can't possibly get much worse."

He watched her move out of his range of vision, which wasn't far since his glasses were in a crumpled, shattered heap on the concrete. As she became nothing more than a blur, he willed her to turn back just once so he could see her pretty features one last time. She didn't oblige him, her walk never faltering, and when she turned the corner, Hal let out a sigh that seemed to come all the way from his toes.

Why couldn't he meet an attractive woman like that without making an utter ass of himself? Gathering his gym bag, he thought about trying to call her, offer to take her to dinner as a way to make up for knocking her over.

A great idea, he thought, *if only I'd learned her name.*

CHAPTER 2

"I'd like a slice of the chocolate cake and a pot of tea. Two cups, please," Lili told the girl behind the counter. "And that popcorn smells too good to resist. A small bag."

Lili found a table and started eating. The clock on the wall opposite her said ten to eight. She'd made the appointment for seven-thirty. Ms. Whitehead had assured her the escorts were all extremely punctual. Except, it seemed, for Hal.

It wasn't too late to cancel. She could just pay for her food to go and walk away before he even showed up. Bubbe and Zayde's anniversary week wouldn't start until next weekend. She had plenty of time to think up some excuse as to why her phantom fiancé was absent from yet another Alster family gathering.

The problem was that she was running out of excuses. Last Thanksgiving had seen her in the Bahamas with her college roommate, Kasey Arlin. Hanukkah had been too far away from Christmas last year for her company's annual break to coincide, and New Year's had been spent with her brother Elijah's family. Their tiny house barely confined Eli and Sarah's rambunctious four kids, so dragging a boyfriend along would have been out of the question, even if she'd really had one to drag.

Now it was already October again, with another round of expected family gatherings looming and no real reason not to show up with her alleged boyfriend in tow.

"Bring him, bubbeleh, for the week," Bubbe Esther had told her every time they spoke on the phone. "What...he's so busy he can't meet his future grandmother-in-law?"

It wasn't that Lili didn't want a boyfriend. In theory, having a companion was a great idea. But when it came right down to it, Lili didn't have the patience or desire to give herself to anyone the way Ian had forced her to give herself to him. It frightened her to take that risk again, though she knew it unlikely she'd end up with a man as manipulative and demanding as Ian Soloman. Still, she hadn't been able to do more than share a single date with any one man in the three years since Ian's death.

It drove her family crazy, and they never ceased pestering her about her love life. Finally, in desperation, Lili had promised her grandmother that she would arrive at the Poconos resort with a man. Once Bubbe got on the phone with Lili's mother, the news spread like wild-fire through the family. They were all expecting to meet him.

If she showed up without him—suffice to say they'd never leave her alone about her love life again. No, the simplest thing, she'd decided was to bring "her man" along and stage a spectacular break up. That would buy her some time. Then when someday, finally, she really did have a boyfriend to bring home, they'd all be so relieved they wouldn't bother picking him apart.

She checked the clock again. Eight o'clock. If he wasn't here in fifteen minutes, she'd take it as a sign from above that she wasn't meant to have a LoveMatch.

She finally caught sight of him out of the corner of her eye. He stood in the Coffeehouse's corner doorway, his glasses steamed from stepping from the chilly October air into the heated room. His head swayed side to side, looking for her.

Something about him seemed so familiar. His stance, the way he combed his hair, the way his hands tugged nervously at his jacket zipper. There was more to it than merely having seen his picture, but Lili couldn't quite figure out what it was.

He took off his glasses to rub them with the tail of his shirt. Recognition startled her into knocking over her teacup. It was the man from yesterday. The one who'd knocked her over in the alley.

"Oh, no," she muttered. It was useless to hope it wasn't him because, when he slipped his glasses back on his nose, his face matched the photo in Ms. Whitehead's binder.

As the tea dripped off the table and her earthenware mug clattered loudly on the floor, the sound caught Hal's attention. She saw him take another quick glance around the room, then head straight toward her. Mopping up the spilled drink with a pile of napkins, Lili kept her head down.

"Uh—Miss Alster?"

She took a deep breath and wiped her fingers with the soggy napkin. "Yes. And you must be—"

"Harold—Hal." He slid into the chair across from her and kicked her cup halfway across the room as he did so. "Uh—sorry."

"I can get another one." How long was it going to take him to recognize her?

He shrugged off his jacket and settled himself on the red vinyl seat, nervously clearing his throat. "I apologize for being late. My car had some problems and I had to get a cab." He stopped abruptly, as though someone had clapped a hand across his mouth. "You!"

"I could say the same thing," Lili remarked. She held out her hand for him to shake.

He reached across the table to take her proffered hand. His sleeve dipped into the remnants of chocolate icing. When he let go of Lili's hand and returned his arm to his side, the mess slopped onto his formerly white oxford shirt.

"You just got—oh, boy." Lili handed another wad of napkins to the oblivious Hal, who hadn't even noticed the stain on his shirt or sleeve. "Hal, you are a real mess, aren't you?"

"I am, I am," he answered ruefully. He took the napkins from her and succeeded in smearing the glop on his shirt even further. With a heavy sigh, he threw the pile of soiled paper on the table. "It's no use. I should just go."

"No!" Lili surprised herself by saying. Despite his clumsiness, his obvious awkwardness, she wanted him to stay. She was desperate.

"No?"

"No," she said firmly. She handed him the glass of water she hadn't planned on drinking and a handful of fresh napkins. "Use this. It might help."

Lili suddenly didn't know what else to say. She barely dated, much less hired men to pretend to be in love with her. Something about the situation made her normal confidence disappear until she felt as awkward as Hal looked.

"Do you come here often?" The line would have been a cliché out of anyone else's mouth. From Hal it merely rang with straightforward interest.

"Sometimes," Lili replied. "I love tea."

He looked at the pot. "It gives me indigestion."

"Oh."

Now they simply stared at each other, the dim lighting painting both of them with shadows. Hadn't Ms. Whitehead said that all LoveMatch's escorts were masters in the art of conversation? Lili was beginning to see why Ms. Whitehead had given her this night for free.

"Miss Alster—"

"Call me Lili."

He smiled. He did have a nice smile, just as she'd earlier thought.

"Lili. Ms. Whitehead said you were looking for an escort to take you on vacation?"

"Not exactly." Lili toyed with her unused fork. "My grandparents are having the family get together for a week at a resort in the Poconos to celebrate their sixtieth wedding anniversary."

"Great!" Hal said enthusiastically.

She eyed him over her squashed cake. "They think I'm engaged."

"And you want me to pretend to be your fiancé."

No matter what else he is, he isn't dumb. "Yes. I'm the only child left in my family who isn't married."

"What about your parents?" He interrupted, taking out a small notepad and pen from his pocket.

"My dad passed away two years ago, but Mom is still in good health. The party is for my dad's folks." Bemused, she watched him write that down.

"Siblings?"

"Three brothers and a sister. I'm the second youngest."

He wrote that down, too, then looked up at her earnestly. "And your family is pressuring you to get married."

"You guessed it."

"So you've been telling them you have a boyfriend for a while now, and they're expecting to meet him. You need me to spend the week acting like an idiot, then break up with you so they'll leave you alone."

Lili nodded, impressed how quickly he figured out the situation. "Is my plan that transparent?"

Hal shook his head. "In my business, we hear a lot of stories."

She wanted to ask him what kind of stories, but didn't. Maybe she didn't really want to know. "Do you think you can handle the job?"

Hal put the notepad and pen down on the table very carefully. His face was serious when he met her eyes. "Lili, why, out of all the escorts in the LoveMatch files, did you pick me? I know that most of the men who work for my company are much—better."

"I picked you because you have a kind face." Lili's answer surprised even herself, but it was worth it when she saw Hal's smile again.

"If you don't mind my asking," he said. "Why don't you have a real boyfriend?"

"I did. He died." The blunt words tumbled from her mouth without grace, but the story wasn't one she could tell delicately. "He was in a car accident three years ago."

"I'm sorry."

"It's okay," Lili said, because telling him the truth—that she wasn't particularly sorry— sounded too cold when spoken aloud. "It was easier to go to LoveMatch."

"And you picked me? I'm a klutz," Hal said with naked honesty. "I always mess up. Half the time I can't even remember to make sure I'm wearing socks that match." He stuck his leg up on the table. "See? This one's blue. The other one's black, I'll bet ten dollars."

"I believe you." Lili laughed. "I'd say you're all the more perfect for my purposes then, right? My family wouldn't expect me to marry a total fool, would they?"

She'd meant her answer lightly, but the way his smile tightened showed she'd stung him. "I didn't mean it that way."

He shrugged, then pointed at his stained shirt. "It's true. But, Lili, I need this job. I need the money. If I screw up one more time, Muriel said she'd have to let me go. I promise you, that if you agree to hire me, I'll be the biggest fool you could ask for."

"Then you're hired," Lili said.

"You won't regret it, I promise," Hal said eagerly. As he reached across the table to shake her hand, he knocked over the pot of tea.

Regret her decision? As the liquid splashed across Lili's thighs, she wondered if she'd survive it.

* * *

In the LoveMatch course on vacation preparation, Hal had learned to pack like a woman. Just making sure he had a baseball cap and enough clean underwear for most of the trip wasn't acceptable, not for one of Muriel Whitehead's "boys." Muriel insisted the LoveMatch escorts lucky enough to be taken on trips be prepared for every contingency. Hal, who'd proudly earned the rank of Eagle Scout, had taken Muriel's instructions to heart.

"We're only going for a week, Hal." Lili watched him manhandle his huge suitcase down the short flight of steps in front of the LoveMatch offices. Her own compact duffle bag and tote were already snuggled together in the trunk of her Volvo S80.

"I wasn't sure if things were going to be formal or not."

Hal lifted his bag into her trunk, almost expecting the car to wheeze under its weight. Maybe he'd been a little overenthusiastic, but this was his first LoveMatch vacation. His first vacation, actually, since he'd quit the accounting firm and started back to school.

He caught her staring at him, but couldn't read her look. "You didn't give me many details."

"Did you pack jeans and a tee-shirt?" Lili asked.

"Yes."

"And something warmer than that—" She pointed to his lightweight windbreaker. "—for night time?"

"Sure did!"

She smiled at him, and the way the expression lit up her eyes took his breath away. "Then you're all set. I don't know what else you've got in there, but you sure are prepared."

"A LoveMatch escort is always prepared," he said.

"Just like the Boy Scouts."

"Just like."

She cocked her head, the wonderful smile still playing about her full mouth. "You're not what I expected from a LoveMatch escort, Hal."

She didn't give him time to answer, as if he had one. He wasn't what most women expected from an escort. Lili motioned to him to get in the car as she slid into the driver's seat. Once inside, Hal leaned back against the leather seat. Her car smelled like vanilla, and suddenly his stomach rumbled.

That earned him a sideways glance from her as she buckled her seatbelt. "Hungry?"

"No, not really." It was a lie. He was starving. He'd depleted his savings several months ago, and paying for tuition and supplies was more important than eating. He'd been living on stale saltine crackers and thrice-used tea bags between LoveMatch checks.

"There's a cooler in the back, if you want something."

His stomach goinged again, louder this time. "Thanks."

"My mother would keel over and die if she thought I left on a trip without taking snacks along with me. I think she's afraid I'm going to

get stranded somewhere and starve to death on the side of the road."
Lili's laugh was warm and smooth. Like honey.

"Mine, too," Hal said. He reached back and hooked the cooler with
his hand, popping open the lid. "Whoa."

Her eyes left the road long enough to shoot him a glance. "Whoa,
what?"

"There's a lot of food in there." To tell the truth, his mouth was
watering just looking at it.

"Help yourself."

Hal saw no reason not to, not when she'd made the offer. He dove
in, sliding a thick tuna sandwich out of its plastic baggie and biting into
it. A thick glop of tuna and mayonnaise slid out from between the slices
of bread and landed on his shirt.

"I packed extra napkins," Lili said.

Hal could only nod as he wiped his shirt. His mouth was too full of
food to reply.

"I guess I'd better go over everything with you before we get
there," Lili began. "Do you need to get your notebook?"

"Right here." He took it from his jacket pocket and uncapped the
pen.

Lili sighed with her mouth pursed upward, so the fringe of her dark
brown bangs blew up from her forehead. "Where should I start?"

"What's my name?"

She shot another quick glance at him. "David Mulder."

Hal wrote down the name. "Interesting."

Lili's full mouth turned down in a frown. "My mother asked me
when I was watching a rerun of *The X-Files*. I was caught off guard."

"Do I look like a David?"

Traffic had slowed to a stop at a bottleneck, and Lili took the
moment to look at him fully. Her gaze was frank and assessing, her
expression serious. Now he could see that the eyes he'd so admired
were not brown as he'd first thought, but a deep, rich caramel. Why
was everything about her reminding him of food?

"No," she said finally. "You look like a Hal. But for this week
you'll be a David anyway."

"And how did we meet?"

"Six months ago, you came to a meeting at my office and asked me
out to dinner. We've been together ever since."

He knew, from the information sheet she'd filled out for
LoveMatch, that she worked for Concentric Health Care. "So I'm an

17

insurance agent?"

"Oh, no." Lili shook her head, making her sleek hair bounce around her shoulders. "You're a doctor."

How was he going to pull that off? "As in MD?"

"Of course. You think I'd marry anything less?" Her tone was light and self-mocking, but he detected an undertone of sadness to it.

"Okay. So I'm Dr. Dave. What kind of doctor am I?" Hal's hand was getting a cramp from writing all this down.

"Proctologist."

"What?" He paused in his writing. "Never mind."

"I've given them the idea you're a nice, upstanding citizen, but not much more information than that." Lili sighed.

I can show them my bar mitzvah picture if they want."

"Your—" She stopped and gave him a glance. "You're Jewish?"

"Is that a problem?"

"No. It's perfect. When you see my family, you'll understand. So what's a nice Jewish boy like you doing as a male escort anyway?" Lili asked as they took the highway out of the city.

"I wanted the chance to bring some joy into the hearts of lovely ladies like yourself," he said, giving the patent LoveMatch answer.

Lili snorted. "And your real reason is?"

"I need the money," Hal admitted. "But don't tell Muriel I told you."

"Your secret is safe with me."

He liked her sense of humor. "And I do like meeting women like you."

He could tell by the way her hands tightened on the steering wheel that he'd touched a nerve. "You mean desperate ones?"

"You don't look desperate to me," he told her.

Lili sighed. "Well, I am. I love my family, God knows, but I'm just tired of The Question."

He could hear the words capitalized in her tone. "The Question?"

"'When are you going to settle down, give us some more grandchildren?'" Lili sighed again, irritably, tapping her fingers on the wheel. "Don't they know it's not that easy?"

"But you want to get married," Hal offered.

"Sure," Lili said. "Who doesn't?"

"Lots of people don't."

"Don't you?"

He shrugged. "I'd have to give up LoveMatch."

Now she laughed out loud again. "Heaven forbid."

"I was married once," Hal said. The admission surprised him. His marriage to Cassie wasn't something he usually talked about.

Lili wasn't laughing any more. She cleared her throat. "Oh?"

"It—it didn't work out," Hal said stiffly.

Lili knew when to back off. They drove in silence for a few minutes. Hal wrapped up his sandwich. Suddenly he didn't feel like eating any more.

*   *   *

By the time they'd pulled into the long driveway of the lodge where the family celebration was taking place, Lili's shoulders and neck ached from the long drive. They were two hours late. She never should have let Hal play navigator. Men were notoriously bad at admitting they were lost. Hal, apparently, was all male.

She parked at the main building, a lovely Victorian mansion hung with twinkling icicle lights. Now her entire body was tense with the thought of actually trying to make this work. She might be able to fool her brothers, and maybe her sister. Possibly even her mother, who was just so glad to hear she had found someone. But fool Bubbe Esther? The woman was eighty years old and still as sharp as a tack.

"Are you going to be all right?"

Hal squeezed her hand. The unexpected warmth of his fingers against hers sent a tingling shock all the way to her toes. The kindness in his question made her throat feel thick with teary gratitude.

She shook it off and extricated her hand. "We might as well get it over with. Are you ready?"

He nodded. "When you are."

"They'll probably all be inside…waiting." She made no move to open the car door and get out. Lili leaned back in her seat and closed her eyes, gathering her strength.

"C'mon," Hal said. "They can't be that bad."

"You'll see," Lili said.

Hal's response was gentle. "Not if we don't get in there."

He was right. She opened one eye to peek at him. "I hope LoveMatch is paying you enough to get through this week."

"It will be my pleasure, I'm sure."

His reply could have sounded smarmy or insincere, but Lili found herself believing him. His words sent another warm tingle through her. Despite the way he seemed to attract destruction, she was very glad she'd picked him instead of muscle-bound Rick.

They got out of the car together and stared up the short but steep flight of stairs to the wraparound front porch. In warmer weather, it would be nice to sit on the rockers up there, but Lili shivered at the thought of sitting outside tonight. It was getting downright cold.

Lili led the way, readying herself for the onslaught she expected as soon as they stepped through the etched glass doors. *I love my family*, she reminded herself. And they meant well. And she didn't want to disappoint them, which was why she was why she'd hired Hal in the first place. So why did she feel so guilty?

Just before they entered the hotel, Hal tucked her hand into his. Before she had time to feel uncomfortable with the sudden, intimate contact, he'd tugged her forward. Inside.

"Lilith, *bubbeleh!*" Bubbe Esther rose from where she'd been holding court in the luxuriously appointed lobby. "You made it!"

"Finally," said Lili's brother Eli from his place at the bar. He tipped a mug of what Lili knew had to be cider toward her. "We've been waiting dinner on you for hours!"

"Hush," Lili's mother Irene scolded her oldest child. "She's here now."

"Come in, come in," called Zayde Saul from Esther's side. "Warm yourselves up.It's colder than a witch's you-know-what out there."

Even though her other siblings and their families weren't there, the crowd seemed overwhelming. For a fleeting moment, Lili wanted to turn and run. She'd never make them believe Hal was her fiancé, and she'd disappoint them all. Then Hal slipped his hand from hers and put his arm around her shoulders. Squeezing her. Giving her unspoken support.

"And so, who's this handsome man with you, huh?" Esther demanded regally. She tipped her head to look over her glasses at him. "Introduce us already."

"Bubbe, Mom, everyone," Lili said. "This is David Mulder, my—my—" That was it. She was choking on the words.

"I'm the lucky man Lili has agreed to marry," Hal said smoothly. He stepped forward to shake Saul Alster's hand. Lili's grandfather returned the shake with a hearty clap on Hal's shoulder.

Her family swarmed around him, descending on him like the biblical plague of locusts. Hal shook hands, endured teasing comments and generally made his way through the massive group by smiling and nodding. Watching him, Lili began to breathe easier. It was going to be all right. Hal was charming them already.

"Lil, I'm glad you finally brought your mystery man to meet us. Mom and I were beginning to think you'd invented him." Lili's sister Ruth smiled to show she was just teasing and gave her a one-armed squeeze. She nodded toward Hal, now being grilled by their brother, Michael, and his wife, Hannah.

Lili's laugh was brief. "As if!"

Ruth shrugged. "Well, I'm just glad you brought him. It's going to be a great week! The kids are all so anxious to meet their new uncle."

Like the kids have a clue, Lili thought, but fondly. Ruth's two boys Henry and Noah were four and six respectively. Even as she thought their names, they hurtled themselves from across the room toward her.

"Aunt Lili!"

She rocked backward from the force of their enthusiastic greeting then knelt to hug and kiss them both. "You smell like chlorine."

"We were swimming," Henry said solemnly.

Noah grinned, showing missing spaces where he'd lost teeth. "The pool is just the coolest, Aunt Lili! It's got buckets that fill up and pour out right on your head!"

"Sounds fun," she said and grabbed each of them for another kiss and hug.

"We're starving," Henry told her. "You taked forever to get here."

"Now you sound like Uncle Eli." Lili ruffled each boy's head and stood again. "Go find your cousins."

Noah wrinkled his nose. "Oh, those girls."

Lili laughed and tweaked his nose. When the boys rushed off, Hal suddenly appeared by her side. He was still smiling, so the first introductions couldn't have been too bad.

"Hi, honey," he said and slipped his hand into hers again. This time the feeling of his fingers against hers didn't seem so strange. In fact, Lili was growing to enjoy this casual contact. It had been a long time since anyone other than a child had held her hand.

"Dinner!" Bubbe Esther was calling to everyone. "Let's eat!"

Hal's stomach rumbled and Lili squeezed his hand. "I hope you're hungry. It's apt to be quite a spread."

"Always." Hal's fingers squeezed hers back.

For a minute, his eyes locked on hers and all Lili could do was stare back at him. Funny, but she hadn't noticed that behind his glasses was a pair of vivid green eyes sparkling with good humor. *Kind eyes. And,* she thought with a bit of shock, *sexy eyes.*

"Wait, Lili." Esther waved the others into the dining room. "You two can't go to the dining room dressed like that. This place is classy."

The old lady grinned and indicated her sparkling, sequined dress. "See? They even got me all duded up. You'll have to change. Why don't you two head down to your room and put something else on? We can wait a few more minutes."

"If that's what you want us to do," Hal said graciously.

Esther reached up and pinched his cheek. "Such a nice boy. Already you know how to kiss up to Bubbe Esther. Smart!"

"All right," Lili agreed. "We'll check into our rooms—"

"Room," Bubbe Esther said.

"Bubbe?" Lili frowned.

"We just got you one, *bubbeleh.* This place is full for the whole week with everyone here, and we had to conserve space. So we figured, you're a grown woman now. With a fiancé." Esther sent another smile to Hal. "Your Zayde and I are modern thinkers. It's all right with us!"

But it wasn't all right with Lili. Holding hands and calling each other honey was one thing…but sharing a room? She could say nothing about it, though, because any protests would sound strange.

"Thanks, Bubbe," she said instead, and pressed a kiss to her grandmother's wrinkled cheek. "We'll go change."

"Those great grandkids of mine are running on candy and caffeine. *Oy!* Their poor parents. They're driving us all *meshuggeneh!*" Esther winked. "Don't get sidetracked."

With that last comment, she swept away toward the dining room.

Sidetracked? Lili wanted to crawl into the ground and die. Getting sex advice from her grandmother had to be the lowlight of her love life. She dared not look at Hal. With burning cheeks, Lili led the way to the main desk to check in.

To their room. Room!

CHAPTER 3

Dinner was chaos and cacophony. Lili's family was loud, affectionate and boisterous. The kids—five nephews and seven nieces—flung food when they thought they could get away with it and whapped each other with their napkins when they thought they couldn't. Her brothers and sister argued back and forth over childhood memories. Her mother refused to take sides. And over it all, Bubbe and Zayde reigned like royalty.

Hal loved every minute of it. As an only child of only children, he hadn't grown up with family all around. Even though he knew this was just a job, a sham, it was nice to pretend for a few hours that he belonged to this family. Besides, with all that was going on, nobody seemed to notice or care he was just as accident prone as the children.

"Get some sleep," Esther was saying to everyone. "Tomorrow, the real fun starts!"

Ruth carried her son Henry, whose eyes were bleary with sleep. "I hope you like being run ragged, David. My grandmother is notorious for planning fun-packed vacations."

"I'm sure it's going to be great." Hal ruffled Henry's hair. "Good night, Henry."

The little boy smiled sleepily and Ruth laughed. "See you in the morning."

Though he'd sat next to Lili during dinner, they hadn't had much time to talk. Now the lobby slowly quieted as people returned to their rooms or sought out further entertainment at the lodge's nightly show.

Lili sank down into one of the overstuffed chairs by the fireplace, which now crackled with flames.

In the orange light, her dark hair gleamed with red and gold highlights. She stared pensively into the flames, her chin in her hand. Hal took a seat across from her.

"So," he said, then faltered. He knew he should start the conversation using one of the pre-approved LoveMatch topics, but nothing seemed appropriate when Lili looked so thoughtful. "Your family seems nice."

She glanced around the room, checking to see if they were alone before replying. "They're great. They're just a little too involved with my life."

Hal thought about his own parents, divorced now for ten years, and the way his phone never rang from either one of them. "You make that sound like a bad thing."

Lili sighed. "I just wish they'd understand that my life is mine is all. I'm not any more thrilled that I'm not married with kids than they are—but I am more resigned to it."

"You sound like you don't think you'll ever get married."

She picked at some threads on her sweater. "It's hard meeting the right person."

She must really have loved her boyfriend, Hal thought, and decided to lighten the mood.

"That's why there's LoveMatch," he said with a grin. "We make it easy for you."

She cast him a dubious look. "Sure, if you're willing to pay for him. Don't tell me any of the clients actually end up marrying the escorts."

"Not usually, no," he admitted. "But then, most of the women who come to LoveMatch aren't looking for a husband."

"No, I guess not." She sat back in the chair, and now the firelight made flickering shadows of her eyes. "It's late. We should go to bed."

He knew she meant her words in the most innocent of ways, but they still made his stomach twist. She'd hired him only to pretend he loved her, but he wondered what it would really be like in Lili's arms. She was by far the prettiest client he'd ever had with her sleek dark hair and clear brown eyes. Her mouth, generous in proportion to her other small features, was now pursed in a tiny grimace he thought might be trepidation. She was thinking about sharing the room.

They'd only been in the room for the ten minutes before dinner that it took to change their clothes. Lili had changed in the bathroom, Hal in the main room. He hadn't had time to really check it out thoroughly, but one thing he knew for sure. One room, one bed.

"It is late," Hal said. "And your sister mentioned something at dinner about horseback riding tomorrow morning? Early?"

"Oh, yeah," Lili said distractedly. She stood. "We'd better go."

From the main lodge, they followed the brick path through well-tended grounds and passed the other lodge buildings until they reached theirs. Each room opened to the outside. When Lili slipped the old fashioned key into the door and swung it open, she paused at the threshold. From behind her, Hal couldn't see her expression, but the way she squared her shoulders before entering told him she was still feeling nervous. Lili carefully put the key on the table just inside the door and paused awkwardly before crossing to the Victorian love seat and sitting.

"Well," she said. "Um."

He sat down beside her so she'd have to look at him. Was it his imagination, or did she shrink slightly away? Hal's courses at LoveMatch had played just this scenario, but it had been a seduction scene. Somehow, he doubted that's what Lili had in mind.

"I'll sleep here on the couch," he offered.

Her look of relief was almost tangible. "Yes, that would be best."

Disappointment panged him. If Lili had hired Rick, nobody would be sleeping on the couch. Or sleeping much at all, Hal was pretty sure.

"Do you want to use the bathroom first?"

"Thanks." She smiled. "For everything. But it's only going to get harder as the week goes on."

Seeing the curve of her lips, Hal knew she was right about that. But not for the reasons she thought. Dealing with Lili's family was going to be easy. Being this close to her without wanting her was going to be torture.

* * *

The bathroom had no shower, only a charming clawfoot tub painted with vivid pink roses. The entire room echoed the pink rose theme with Victorian cherub prints on the wall and pale pink rosebud wallpaper. The toilet was the old-fashioned kind with a pull-chain, and the pedestal sink had lovely, old porcelain fixtures.

It was the sort of bathroom Lili would thoroughly enjoy…if she hadn't been so caught up thinking about the man waiting for her just outside the door. Quickly, she washed her face and brushed her teeth, then slipped on the flannel boxers and oversized tee-shirt she wore for pajamas. She scolded herself when she caught herself thinking she wished she had something a little more feminine.

"I didn't hire him to be my lover," she muttered as she pulled her hair back in a ponytail. "Just to pretend to be."

She was ready. Her hand hesitated on the doorknob. *Hal is a nice man,* she told herself. *A professional.* Ms. Whitehead had assured her that hiring a LoveMatch escort meant complete peace of mind. He would behave appropriately at all times. What seemed appropriate was entirely up to her.

Was that what was bothering her? That she knew Hal wouldn't make a move on her? Or that he would, but only as part of his job, and only if she gave him the right signals?

Lili shoved such thoughts away firmly. Hal was a nice guy, if a bit clumsy, and so what if he had sexy eyes and a great smile? She was paying him to be interested in her and that was all.

"It's all yours." She brushed by him, head held high.

He took a small case and a bundle of clothes from his ridiculously large bag and went into the bathroom. Through the closed door Lili could hear water running and the toilet flushing. Gargling. Her cheeks pinked. There wouldn't be much privacy this week.

She found some extra blankets and pillows in the large carved armoire and laid them on the love seat. She looked down at Hal's new bed critically. He was at least six-two . Most of him would be hanging over the edge. She looked at the large, luxuriously appointed brass bed.

No. She couldn't invite him to join her. She looked again at the love seat, with its scratchy buttons and hard cushions. But could she sleep on that?

She was saved from self-sacrifice when the bathroom door opened and Hal came out. He'd slicked his wheat-colored hair back from his forehead in smooth waves. He wore only a pair of loose cotton drawstring pants, but it wasn't his bare feet that made Lili's breath catch in her throat. It was his bare chest.

Beneath the oxford shirts, Hal had been hiding the chest of a real David. Michaelangelo's David, to be more precise. His skin was smooth and nearly golden in the room's dim lighting. His abs were sculpted, his pecs smooth humps of muscle sprinkled with just a smattering of crinkly golden hair. His arms, too, bulged with well-defined muscle, but none of it was grotesque or overblown. He didn't look like a body-builder, just like a man who took care of himself.

"I left my t-shirt in the suitcase," he said apologetically.

Lili swallowed hard, willing the saliva pooling in her mouth to moisten her dry throat. All she could think was, *Whoa.* Her mind called up an image of Clark Kent and Superman. What else was Hal hiding behind his glasses and his slightly geeky wardrobe? The phrase Man of Steel rose to her mind and made her blush at the implications.

She stepped aside to let him open his suitcase. The huge bag was too big to rest comfortably on the room's small suitcase stand. Hal wrestled with the bag, finally managing to balance it on the stand. Lili watched in guilty pleasure as his muscles tensed and strained under the weight.

"Just a minute." Hal fiddled with the suitcase's zipper. It didn't budge. Hal pulled harder, really tugging on it with strength.

Lili saw that when he'd zipped the bag earlier, he'd caught a piece of clothing in it. The way he was working at the zipper now, he'd never be able to open it. "Let me help you."

Everything happened all at once. Lili moved next to Hal and slipped her fingers into the small opening, freeing the caught cloth. Hal's tugging released the zipper forcefully. The suitcase lid, bulging with all the stuff Hal'd packed, flew open. Hal fell backward, knocking Lili over with him. She landed on his chest with an, "Oof!" The suitcase, set precariously on the stand fell over on top of both of them.

Lili had just a few seconds to appreciate the warmth of Hal's bare skin against her cheek and the way he smelled before the square silver packets rained down on them both. There were dozens of them, some larger, some smaller, but all contained the same thing.

"Condoms?" Lili cried, holding one in her hand. Extra-ribbed for her pleasure.

She threw herself off of Hal, stepping on him in the process. Hal let out a low, pained groan and curled into a fetal position. Lili barely noticed the damage she'd caused. She flung the prophylactic down with the rest of them, and it hit Hal squarely in the head.

"Condoms?" She looked around at the mess from Hal's suitcase, noticing the sheer extravagant number of them. "I don't know what you were thinking, mister, but—"

"...prepared," Hal wheezed.

Lili noticed he was cupping his privates. *Oops.* "What did you say?"

Hal managed to sit up, but his face had gone pale. "We have to be prepared for anything. That's the LoveMatch rule."

"So, along with your three changes of clothing per day, you thought you'd better pack condoms." Lili stepped over the suitcase and flopped down on the bed. "Some Eagle Scout!"

"I'm sorry," Hal said. He began shoving things back in his bag. "I wasn't sure if—"

"If what?" Lili demanded. "If I'd be so horny or lonely that I'd beg you to service me?"

He didn't answer right away, and she thought she'd embarrassed him.

"I just didn't know. And I didn't want to be in a situation where I might regret not taking precautions. That's all."

She'd known many men who expected an evening to end up in sex but didn't bother with thinking about protection. Maybe she'd overreacted. But she didn't know how to say she was sorry to the man who now, silently, had taken his place on the love seat.

"Goodnight," she said finally, and turned off the light. In the light coming in through the window, dozens of little silver packets gleamed on the carpet.

So many of them. How many had he expected to need? Again, she thought, *Man of Steel*, and a hot blush stole across her face. *What kind of man was Hal in bed anyway?*

*   *   *

Hal's knees were on fire and his rear end felt like it had been slammed with a crowbar. The slow, plodding animal between his legs was no rodeo champion, no thoroughbred racer. Just a slow, placid horse who liked to follow the others on the trail in front of him. Without stopping. For hours.

The ride had begun at sunrise. The whole family, all but the youngest kids, gathered at the stable to get their mounts and head out into the rolling hills and woods of the resort's property. Hal's last ride had been on a pony. He'd been six.

"How're you doing? All right?" Lili urged her horse, a black-and-white mare named Daisy, next to Hal's mount, Stanley.

"Oh, sure," Hal said through gritted teeth. "Just fine."

Lili walked her horse beside him for a few minutes. The others on the ride kept their faster pace, but Hal could see another patch of rough meadow opening up in front of them and was grateful Lili had slowed them to a walk.

"You're doing great for a beginner," she said encouragingly.

Stanley paused to put his head down and pull at some of the weeds growing by the trail side. Hal pulled on the reins. Stanley ignored him.

"Don't let him eat," Lili said.

"I'm not letting him do anything," Hal muttered. He yanked the reins again, hard, and Stanley started moving again.

"The ride's almost over." Lili smiled at him.

Suddenly, he no longer felt the pain in his legs and butt.

"Then we can hit the tennis courts."

Was she trying to kill him? All Hal wanted to do after this ride was soak for a while in the hot tub. A long while. But he wasn't on vacation; he was working. And his job was to do whatever Lili wanted him to do.

Still, his face must have shown his true feelings, because Lili laughed. "I'm kidding. I'm thinking that a big breakfast, followed by a nice long soak in the whirlpool is in order."

Hal sent a prayer up to the powers that be. "I'm at your service."

Wrong choice of words. He remembered her comment of the night before about if he'd expected to service her, and he wished he'd thought of that before speaking. Lili frowned a little and lifted her chin, focusing her eyes back on the trail ahead instead of on him.

"All work and no play," she said quietly. "You know how it goes. I know this is a job for you, Hal, but it's okay if you want to enjoy yourself."

Why on earth would she think he wouldn't enjoy food and a soak in the hot tub? No matter how many of the LoveMatch training courses he took, Hal knew he'd never understand women. He sat back a little in the saddle, trying to ease the pressure on his knees.

"I'm enjoying myself." The lie flew out of him like a sneeze.

Lili looked at him skeptically. "Sure you are."

"I haven't ridden very much, that's all." There was no way he was going to mention to her that he felt like the entire lower half of his body was going to split right in two.

"My family's been coming here to Bramblewood since before I was born. My grandparents had their honeymoon here." Lili ducked to escape a low-hanging clump of branches. They were entering another patch of trees. "This is the first time I've been here in about four or five years, though."

Hal rocked in the saddle again to ease the pressure. "What kept you away?"

"Oh, you know." Lili kept her eyes on the trail ahead. "I was busy with my job, didn't get vacation right away, moved into a new apartment. Stuff like that."

He could tell by the tense set of her jaw that there was more to her story, and suspected it might have something to do with the boyfriend who'd died. He also knew better than to push her. Creating casual conversation wasn't one of his better skills, and diving into a topic that so obviously upset her would only be asking for trouble.

"I do love my family," she said almost defensively. As though he'd insinuated that she didn't. "But they just—they just won't leave me alone."

"They just want to see you happy." Hal knew that without a doubt. Love for each other shone in every Alster face, unlike in his family where holiday dinners had often disintegrated into shouting matches or cold, stony silences.

Lili snorted. "Yeah, I know. And I hate to keep disappointing them."

Despite the sun rising in the sky, the air here was chill with the promise of winter. Under the trees, the shadows were even cooler. Hal was glad he'd packed his thick fleece pullover and pants. The horses plodded along the trail, one sometimes moving slightly ahead of the other, but generally the path was wide enough for them to keep pace.

"You think they're disappointed in you?" He asked. "Because— you're not happy?"

Slashes of sunlight cut through the shadows, and when Lili passed beneath them, they lit her face in bars of black and gold. She'd pulled her thick, dark hair back beneath a baseball cap today. Her deep purple field coat had collar and cuffs of green corduroy, which matched her pants. Instead of cowboy boots, she wore low-heeled brown boots that laced, and she tucked her feet into the stirrups with a practiced ease Hal envied. His own feet, laced into hiking boots, weren't nearly as comfortable.

"Why would you say that?" she asked sharply. Her eyes flashed when she turned to look at him. "I'm happy!"

Hal backed off a little. "Sure. Okay."

She looked back at the trail ahead and kicked her horse to speed it up. "We're almost at the end. They'll be waiting for us."

Stanley, following Daisy, also picked up the pace. Hal groaned as each trotting step forced even more agony into his chafed skin and strained muscles. Lili urged Daisy even faster along the now smooth trail. Hal could see the barn just beyond the curve ahead. Apparently, Stanley could, too, because the massive gelding suddenly broke into a full trot.

All Hal could do was hang on for the ride. The horses seemed to thunder down the dirt path, heading for the corral. Hal could see the others had already begun to dismount or let their horses drink from the huge vats of water placed around the stable yard.

Hal gritted his teeth, gripping as best he could with thighs from which he could no longer feel anything but constant agony. His fingers slipped through the leather reins as Stanley tossed his head, eager to get back to his box and feed. Daisy and Lili were up ahead, already slowing as Lili guided the horse toward one of the mounting blocks.

"Whoa," Hal muttered through grunts of pain. "Whoa!"

Either Stanley didn't hear, or he didn't understand. The horse kept going. Now Hal began to lose sensation in his legs all together as Stanley picked up speed for the last final dash into the corral. The reins slipped again, flopping against the horse's neck in a way that seemed to urge him on even faster.

With one final, heaving effort, Hal managed to gather the reins, grip with his legs, and dig his feet into the stirrups. "Whoa!"

The horse whoa'ed all right, coming to a dead stop that sent clods of earth flying up from its hooves. The problem wasn't that the horse stopped. It was that Hal kept going.

*   *   *

"You're sure lucky you landed in the watering trough," Michael told Hal. He shook his head in male camaraderie and amazement. "Man, I never saw someone fly over a horse's head like that before."

Lili watched Hal force a grin. His mouth was still slightly swollen on the right side from where he'd hit it on the edge of the trough. His eyes were bloodshot.

"I've seen you take some pretty rough tumbles," Michael's wife, Hannah, said from the other side of the table. "And you've landed in worse things than water."

"'member when Uncle Eli fell off into the horse poop?" Henry laughed wildly until orange juice squirted from his mouth.

"Gross, buttwad!" Eli and Sarah's daughter, Rebecca, a worldly nine years old, imitated gagging.

Henry, who pretended with Noah to despise his older, female cousins, closed his mouth. His lower lip trembled. Lili, feeling sorry for her sweet, little nephew, reached over to give him a quick squeeze.

"Don't feel bad, Henry," she said. "I've changed Rebecca's diapers, remember? Talk about gross."

That put a smile back on Henry's face, and he threw a piece of pancake across the table. The table erupted into chaos, as was usual at these family gatherings. Lili couldn't help smiling until she caught a glance of Hal. His expression was strained, though he tried gamely to hide it behind a smile so fake it looked like plastic.

Guilt assailed her. It was partially her fault he'd been thrown. She knew he wasn't a good rider, and she knew Stanley would want to catch up to the other horses if left behind. Suddenly, Lili felt like an ant at a picnic. An undeserving pest.

"C'mon, H—oney," she said. Her cheeks pinked as she realized she'd almost called him Hal instead of David. "Let's get our bathing suits on and go in the hot tub."

Silence circled the table at her statement, then everyone who'd heard her burst into catcalls and kissing noises. Her blush deepened, but she pretended not to be bothered by her family's good-natured teasing.

"Have a good time!" Ruth's husband, Frank, called from a few chairs down. "Don't get overheated!"

The adults laughed, but Henry merely gave her a puzzled look. "But, Aunt Lili, don't you want to get all hot and wet? That's what you do in the hot tub."

Her nephew's innocent remark sent Lili's ears and cheeks into an inferno of blushing. Her siblings nearly choked on their laughter, while her mother pretended to be shocked. Esther had to ask twice what it was Henry said, and when Elijah finally managed to stop laughing long enough to tell her, the old lady's laughter was louder and longer than anyone else's.

Through it all, Hal sat stoically, a fixed grin on his face. Lili made shushing noises, which everyone ignored, and finally saw that nobody was going to stop teasing until she and Hal left. She stood and waited for Hal to do the same. He did so with a stiff dignity she thought meant he was offended.

But how could he be offended? Especially because of what he did for a living? It wasn't until they'd left the others behind in the dining area and had begun the long walk back to their room that Lili realized why Hal was moving like a toy with rusted gears. He was in pain.

She saw it in the shuffle of his feet and the way he clenched his hands at every crack or obstacle he had to maneuver around. She saw it in the beads of sweat lining up on his reddening brow. Every few minutes, his tongue snaked out to swipe across his thinned lips.

"You'd better take some ibuprofen right away," Lili said sympathetically as they finally reached the door to their room.

"No, thanks," Hal said rigidly. He leaned against the doorframe while she fumbled with the key, but couldn't quite get his body to relax enough to make the stance look casual. "I'm fine."

"You don't look fine."

"I'm…fine."

Lili shrugged and opened the door. It took her only a few minutes to change into her bathing suit, a demure tankini in a vivid shade of violet. She pulled on a sweatshirt and a pair of jeans, and went out into the bedroom again.

Hal sat on the loveseat, one leg out of his jeans, but the other still inside. "I can't move."

Pity flooded her. "Let me help you."

He started to protest, but fell quiet as she knelt before him. Lili eased his legs out of the jeans, trying not to notice the firm muscles of his calves or the thick furring of gold-brown hair covering them. She peeled off his white athletic socks. Hal's feet, she didn't want to see, were large but finely boned. He had sexy toes.

Putting her mind firmly back to the task at hand, Lili held out her hand and pulled him to a standing position. Hal groaned at the movement. His shirt, thankfully, fell down to cover him to his thighs, so she was spared the sight of him in his briefs.

"Where's your suit?"

"In my bag."

Silly question. Lili dug around until she found one, an outrageously skimpy black bikini bottom. She held it up. "This?"

Hal groaned again. "Keep looking. That's—the special bathing suit."

Lili couldn't help it. She laughed. "Special for what?"

Hal merely glared at her, and she decided not to press him. She dug around further, pulling out neatly folded stacks of clothing. Hal's suitcase was like Mary Poppins' carpetbag: endless. Finally, she found another suit. This one was normal trunks with a Hawaiian print and drawstring.

"Do you think you can put this on by yourself?"

He nodded, gritting his teeth. "Go. Bathroom."

"Me? Or you?" He gave her another look and Lili felt cruel. "Okay. Just holler when you're ready and I'll come out. And while I'm in there, let me get you some aspirin or something. Please?"

He didn't speak, but only nodded. *Men.* Still, she felt badly for him. Her own thighs and ankles were sore from not riding in a while, and she hadn't been thrown into a watering trough to end the ride. She could only imagine how poor Hal felt.

Several long minutes later, he called that he was ready. Lili left the bathroom and handed him three red pills and a glass of water. "Take these."

He did. He'd managed to get his trunks on, at least, and his jeans. "Can we please go now?

"Can you make it?"

"Yes, Lili, I can make it."

"Just asking," she said.

By the time they'd walked the distance to the outdoor whirlpool, Hal was shaking and he'd taken her hand. Of course, he'd taken it in response to seeing her brother Mark and his wife, Debbie, coming down the path toward them, but he hadn't let go even after they passed. At this time of day, the gazebo and hot tub were deserted, though Lili suspected more than one pair of watchful eyes peeked at them from the windows in the lodge.

Hal sank into the water with a sigh of relief so great it was almost a sob. "Thank God."

"I'm sorry, Hal," Lili said sincerely. "We didn't have to go on the ride this morning."

The hot water seemed to be reviving him because he actually managed a smile. The sheer charm of it made her catch her breath. Lili looked away, concentrating on skimming off her clothes and dipping into the hot water before the cool air could do more than tickle her.

"You mean you didn't tell them I'm a champion rider as well as a champion proctologist?"

"No." Actually, she hadn't told them very much at all, though there'd been plenty of questions. She'd usually managed to duck the more probing ones. "You didn't do so bad."

He raised one eyebrow at her. "If you call getting tossed into a vat of slimy, freezing water not too bad, then I guess you're right."

He had a good sense of humor about himself. Lili liked that. Ian would never have admitted to being anything less than an athletic god. For him to do anything less than perfectly was impossible—at least in his own eyes.

"I hope I'm not interrupting the canoodling," interrupted a booming male voice.

"No, Uncle Ira. Of course not." Lili smiled weakly up at her grandfather's younger brother. "Are you coming in?"

The massive man with the infectious grin chortled. "If you two love birds don't mind."

"Not at all," Hal said. His voice had returned to normal.

The hot tub must be working for him.

"Hey, Myrna! Lou! Yetta! The kids aren't fooling around! C'mon in!"

All at once, the empty hot tub became nearly overcrowded as Lili's aunts and uncles joined them. What had seemed like gallons of water between she and Hal had shrunk to microscopic drops as they were pressed closer to one another to accommodate the crowd.

His thigh, delightfully rough with crinkly hair, slid against her smooth one. His hip nudged hers beneath the bubbling water. His calf—she could feel the muscles she'd so earlier admired—rubbed hers, slipped away, then snuck back again for another stroke. The water caressed them, tickled them, bubbled around and over them, bringing them together and forcing them apart.

Dear Lord, Lili thought somewhat faintly as the steam rose all around her with her family's laughter. *I* am *getting overheated.*

CHAPTER 4

The stint in the hot tub's soothing wonders had done him a world of good, but Hal still winced as he bent to tie his shoes. The ache in his butt and thighs had faded, but his knees grumbled in protest with every movement. A lot of good all those LoveMatch sponsored workouts had done him.

Lili came out of the bathroom, looking fresh in another pair of corduroy pants and a gold colored turtleneck. "Brrrr. Is it cold in here?"

It was a little chilly in the room, but Hal didn't really notice. Looking at Lili made him feel a lot warmer. He finished tying his shoes. "We can check the radiator."

She checked her watch. "We can do that later. It's just about time for the afternoon entertainment to start."

Lili's Bubbe had come by the hot tub earlier and invited all of them to come down for the staff-run entertainment in the main lodge. Apparently, Bramblewood hosted games and ongoing activities to round out its menu of outdoor activities. This afternoon it was some sort of trivia game with prizes. Hal was pretty good at trivia.

Now Lili looked at him and cocked her head to the side in the way he was beginning to recognize as her thoughtful pose. "You look nice."

Her compliment pleased him. He looked down at his jeans, dark green turtleneck and heavy black sweater. "Thanks!"

"You actually match," she said. "But let me see your socks."

Socks. Darn. Hal lifted his pants legs and revealed the socks sticking out of his hiking boots. One black and one dark brown.

Lili laughed. "Why not just buy them all the same color?"

"I thought I did," Hal said ruefully.

She cocked her head at him again, and her eyes drifted over his face, then down his body and up again. A smile formed on the mouth he'd begun finding himself thinking about at inopportune times. Her assessment stirred him in a way that might quickly become uncomfortable or awkward if he didn't do something fast.

"Baseball," Hal blurted. *Was that out loud?*

Lili's dreamy gaze snapped to clarity. Her brow creased. "What?"

"Uh—baseball," Hal said. Well, he didn't have to worry his body's reaction any more. Embarrassment was a great way to quench desire. "Do you like baseball?"

She shrugged. The mood, whatever it had been, had passed. Now she busied herself with slipping her sweater over her head and brushing out her hair. "I guess so. What brought that up?"

Brought up, indeed. "I just wondered if there'd be any baseball trivia at that game today."

"I doubt it." Lili finished her preparations and tucked the key into her pocket. "It's some sort of Bramblewood version of the Newlywed Game."

At least he'd managed to cover himself. "Sounds fun."

"You're being a really great sport about this whole trip," Lili said. To his surprise and pleasure, she reached out to take his hand. "Thanks, Hal."

The touch of her fingers sent an electrical shock all the way down his arm. "I'm paid to please, Lili," he gibbered, barely aware of what was flying out of his mouth.

She withdrew her hand. Her eyes, which had been clear just the moment before, clouded. "Oh, right. Well. Let's go. We don't want to miss anything."

She left ahead of him. Hal allowed himself the guilty pleasure of watching her rear-end roll beneath the sturdy corduroy pants. She caught him looking when she turned unexpectedly.

"What are you doing?"

He had no answer that wouldn't sound just plain stupid. "Nothing."

She hmmphed. The walk to the main lodge led them along a twisting maze of trails through gardens that now bloomed with mums and late fall displays of pumpkins and scarecrows. They passed the hot tub in its gazebo, empty now. The playground looked somehow forlorn with the swings and seesaws removed for the winter.

Hal caught up to her and took her hand. Lili jerked at his touch, but didn't pull away. Ahead of them lay the main lodge, and they could see members of the group heading down other paths toward it.

"Would you rather I didn't hold your hand?" He spoke in a low voice as they approached the steps to the front porch.

"No, no," she said in a tone that sounded forced. "I guess you should. It adds to the realism."

"That's what I thought." What he'd actually thought was that he wanted to feel her skin on his again. Now he was close enough to smell her perfume. *Roses?* As they climbed the steep stairs, he let her move just enough ahead of him that he could bend forward to sniff the fragrance again.

"What are you doing?" Lili's tone was angry, but she was smiling. "Hi, Bubbe!"

Hal turned and saw Esther and Saul on the porch's far side. They waved but didn't come over. Esther pointed inside and Hal nodded. "We'll be there in a minute!"

As soon as Lili's grandparents disappeared into the house, her smile turned down. "Hal?"

"You smell good."

"Oh." His answer seemed to unnerve her. "So you had to sniff me?"

Before he could answer, she'd grabbed him around the neck and pressed her mouth to his. Hal didn't question…he just reacted. Her body against his was solid but curvy beneath her heavy clothes. Her lips were softer even than he'd imagined.

Then, just like that, she pulled away. For another moment, Hal mouthed the air before realizing she was no longer there. "Lili?"

"Sorry to interrupt." Ruth grinned and looked completely unapologetic. "I just wanted to know if you two were coming in."

"We'll be there in just a minute," Lili said.

How had a kiss so brief turned her mouth so red and her hair so mussed?

Ruth nodded and winked at Hal. "We'll be waiting for you. Don't be late."

Lili's sister went into the house. Lili sighed. "Sorry."

He didn't want her to be sorry. He wanted her to kiss him again. Hal understood she'd only kissed him to impress her sister. "Hey, that's what—"

"What you're paid for." Lili frowned. "I know."

He stepped closer to her, pulling her in next to him. She had to tilt her head to look up at him. "Maybe we should practice a little bit more before we go in. You know, just to make it look a little more— realistic."

Hal thought for sure she'd see right through his obvious suggestion. He hadn't overstepped the LoveMatch rules of propriety, but if she said no, he wouldn't be able to ask again, unless she initiated contact. She stared at him so long and with such an expression of concentration he knew she was going to say no and probably fire him in the bargain.

Instead, Lili stepped further into Hal's embrace. "That sounds like a good idea," she said, and offered up her mouth to him again.

* * *

Lili had only kissed him because she'd spotted Ruth heading toward them. The way they stood, with Hal leaning so close to her, looked awkward. Ruth had eyes like a hawk and Lili didn't want her sister to suspect anything, so she kissed him.

The kiss had lasted only a few moments, barely enough time for her to register any sensation. Besides, she'd been so consumed with making it look natural to Ruth there had been no room for anything else. Hal did have a point, though. If they were going to pass for an engaged couple, and one sharing a room no less, they'd better make it look real enough to fool her family.

"You mean it?" he asked her, then seemed to recover. "I mean, yeah. Right."

Why wasn't he kissing her? Why was he just—looking at her? Sudden self-consciousness flooded her and Lili took a step back. She didn't want to think about this, for Heaven's sakes! *Just do it!*

Hal's face took on an expression of determination, and he stepped in to cover the distance she'd created between them. He bent to kiss her. Hesitated. She leaned up as he leaned down. Both of them wavered this time. It was just like being back in junior high, only they were on the front porch of a Victorian mansion instead of somebody's rec room closet.

This close, she could see his green eyes were really hazel, tiny sparkles of gold in them. His broad mouth, which looked much handsomer with a smile on it, had thinned with concentration. He looked like he was going to bite her, not kiss her.

The longer they danced around this, the worse it was going to be. And what if someone saw them? Even worse...was watching them now? They probably both looked like a couple of idiots.

Lili took a deep breath, grabbed Hal by the front of his thick sweater and stood on her toes to reach his mouth. This time they came together in a spectacular crash of teeth against teeth, gums against gums. Lili felt Hal's lips squash on hers. She'd heard of bells ringing during a kiss, but she'd always imagined them sounding like celestial fairy chimes. Not ambulance sirens.

"Er." Hal grimaced. "Whoa."

"Well, that won't do at all," Lili said angrily. She put her hands on her hips and glanced around the porch to make sure they were still alone. "Ms. Whitehead told me you guys took classes and stuff!"

"Hey, wait a minute," Hal said, clearly affronted. He gingerly felt his mouth. "We do. I did. But we don't—we don't take kissing classes!"

"Well, that's obvious," Lili said. She was being unfair, perhaps irrational, but her embarrassment fueled her.

Another look of grim determination slid down over Hal's face. He pulled her against the full length of his body, his fingers gripping her upper arms nearly tight enough to hurt. He bent to her mouth, sliding his lips against hers.

Lili, caught unprepared, didn't have time to take a breath. Or was it the way he smelled that left her gasping for air? Or the way his broad chest felt crushed against hers? Whatever caused the sensations ripping through her, she surrendered to them wholeheartedly.

Hal's mouth was sweet like oranges, his lips plump with passion. They teased her lips, urging them to open. His tongue swiped delicately at hers, once and twice. When she tried to return the gesture, though, all at once he broke away.

Hal stepped away from her so quickly she almost fell without the support of his hands. "I'd say that was better, wouldn't you?"

Lili's knees were still weak, but she recognized a challenge when she heard one. "It was all right. Why don't you let me give it a try?"

The staff had not yet taken down the swing hanging from the porch's beams. Lili put her hands on Hal's chest, pushing him down with a sudden movement so he stumbled to the side. His leg hit the swing and he sat, grabbing for the high back so he wouldn't fall.

Lili followed his movements with her own, sliding her knee onto the swing's seat and bracing herself against the back. Her mouth was on Hal's before he had time to even make a sound. The swing rocked as she kissed him. She made no pretense of tenderness, and he demanded none. There was no hesitation between them this time. His tongue met hers with a strong, swift stroke that twisted and turned her stomach. His free hand reached up and grabbed a handful of her hair, pulling her toward him.

Lili almost lost her balance, but caught herself before falling on him completely by putting her hand on his shoulder. Hal's hand moved to the back of her neck, and his fingers found the sensitive part just behind her ear. The breadth of his shoulder beneath her hand made her slip her fingers down to the even broader expanse of his chest.

Both of them came up for air, breathing heavily. She could feel a flush along her cheeks and knew it continued down her throat and to the first swell of her breasts. Lili's nipples strained against the sheer fabric of her bra.

"Not bad," Hal said hoarsely. "But practice does make perfect."

What am I doing? What am I doing? What am I doing? The question pounded in her mind as Lili watched Hal move in for another kiss. This wasn't supposed to happen. A few pecks on the mouth, a little bit of hand holding, maybe a hug or two just to make sure everyone saw them being affectionate. But making out like teenagers on the front porch swing while, she realized in sudden horror, her nephew Henry looked on from the front parlor window?

"Oh, Lord," she muttered, turning her face before Hal could catch her again.

He must have sensed she wasn't just spouting words of passion because he stopped. "Lili?"

She didn't want to point, so instead she rolled her eyes toward the window. "We have an audience."

Hal glanced there and saw Henry. "Oops."

"We really should go in." Lili looked down and saw that, at some point, her hands had ended up all over him. So had his on her.

She disentangled herself carefully and stood. Hal followed, less quickly, and it took her a long, dumb moment to realize why. When she saw him shift uncomfortably and pull his sweater down over his belt, her blush deepened. At the same time, she couldn't fight the grin that wanted to leap out. Had she affected him that much?

"Aunt Lili, what were you guys doing?" Henry asked when they came in the front door.

"Oh, just—tickling each other," Lili said lightly and ruffled the little boy's hair.

Henry frowned. "It didn't look like you guys were laughing."

She shot Hal a glance. "No, I guess we weren't."

Henry shrugged with a four-year-old's wisdom. "Sometimes, when

Daddy tickles Mommy, she doesn't laugh either. And hey, Aunt Lili, you know what?"

"What?" Lili asked in trepidation, hoping she wasn't going to be unwillingly let in on Ruth and Frank's bedroom habits.

"Chicken butt!" Henry laughed gleefully, slapping his little knee. "You know why?"

"Why?" Lili asked, laughing along with him.

"Chicken thigh!" This really set Henry off into gales of laughter. His small face scrunched up in the sheer pleasure of the joke, and Lili loved him so much she had to suddenly bend down and kiss his sweet, soft cheeks until he yelled and pushed away.

"Yuck," he said resentfully, rubbing away the marks she'd left. "I'm getting out of here!"

Watching him go, Hal smiled. "He's a great kid."

"Yes." Lili sighed. "They all are."

"You'd be a great mom," Hal said.

"Sure." Lili laughed, though she didn't feel like it.

"No, I mean it." Hal took her hand. "You're great with him. With all of them."

"Someday," she said, and stopped. Then shrugged, as though it didn't matter. "Should we find the others?"

Hal nodded. He didn't let go of her hand. They walked down the hall toward the stairs leading to the lodge's lower level. How had something as simple and complicated as a few kisses made holding his hand seem so natural?

*   *   *

"What is your mate's favorite color?" The young man read the question off the card, then looked at the contestants expectantly.

Hal had been able to answer most of the questions so far, hair color, eye color, height. But now he stared at his blank card and fiddled with his pen. *What to answer?* He snuck a glance around at the other men sitting in the folding chairs. All of them were busy scribbling. He was the only one with a blank look on his face. He thought hard, and decided to take a guess. Lili looked good in purple, and he'd noticed she wore it often. Purple, he wrote on the card.

"What is your mate's favorite perfume?" *That's easy. Roses. She smelled like roses.*

"Now here's a hard one, guys. What size shoe does your mate wear?"

At least Hal wasn't the only one with a blank look this time. The crowd laughed and teased as the men who'd gamely agreed to play the Bramblewood game shrugged and scribbled.

"All right, now let's bring out our ladies and have them answer the questions! Whoever gets the most right wins!" The young man, dressed in a pullover with Bramblewood's logo embroidered on it, waved the cards in the air. "Ready?"

The crowd hooted. Bubbe Esther led the ladies in, and they took their seats next to their spouses and boyfriends. Lili's expression was excited, but Hal knew she was faking. Neither of them had volunteered for the game, but had been recruited to fill the last empty slot. He knew she was worried his answers would expose how little he knew about her.

The emcee went down the line, asking all the women to answer the same question. After they gave their answer, their respective partner was supposed to show what he'd written on the card. Most of the men, Hal was relieved to note, got a slap or an outraged squawk when they read their answers.

It was their turn. "Blue," Lili answered confidently when the announcer asked her eye color.

Hal looked at the answer he'd written. "Blue with amazing flecks of gold and green, like ocean waters."

Lili stared at him in amazement. The catcalls and teasing shouts coming from the audience turned to oohs and ahs. The announcer chuckled and gave them the point.

She looked at him again with wonder when he named her perfume, favorite color and shoe size all correctly. That he'd only guessed at the shoes didn't seem to matter. Out of all the couples playing along, Hal was the man who got nearly all the questions right. The only one he missed was her middle name, Eliana, and he'd had no way of even guessing that.

"We have a winner!" The announcer declared when the game ended. "Hal and Lili!"

The family members and strangers in the small room cheered and hollered. Everyone congratulated them. The prize was a weekend for two at Bramblewood. The package included the honeymoon suite with private whirlpool tub, champagne breakfast in the room and a horse and carriage ride, plus dinner at a neighboring gourmet restaurant.

"Lili, it looks like you and David will be coming to Bramblewood for your honeymoon, just like me and Zayde did." Bubbe Esther linked her one arm through each of Lili and Hal's. "*Oy,* sixty years ago. How time passes! I wish the same joy for both of you that your grandfather and I have had, Lili."

"Thanks, Bubbe." Lili accepted Esther's kiss on her cheek.

When the old lady motioned to Hal to bend down and get kissed, too, he did so with a major pang of guilt. He knew he was being paid to deceive these people, but did they all have to be so nice?

"Bubbe, we're going down to the game lounge to shoot some pool!" Some of Lili's teenage cousins crowded around them, jostling for kisses and nose squeezes from Esther.

"Go, go," Esther said, unlinking her arm from Lili's to flap her hand at them. "Enjoy!"

The announcer was setting up the room to start another couples game, but most of the Alster family was leaving for other pursuits. From what Hal had read on the activities menu, there were plenty to choose from. Esther seemed content to walk with them to the cozily decorated fire lounge.

"Sit," she said, indicating the pair of sofas in front of the merrily crackling fire. "I need to get to know my future grandson-in-law a little better."

Hal and Lili sat together. He slipped his arm around her shoulder, trying to make the movement look casual and practiced. The only problem was he didn't know what to do with his fingers. Did she like him to slide them along side her neck or curl them around her upper arm? Was he pulling her too close? Was he choking her?

"David?"

Too late, he realized Esther had asked him a question. "Sorry?"

The old lady laughed, leaning forward on her couch across from them. "That's all right. Lose yourself in my granddaughter's ocean blue eyes. That's what young lovers do, don't you know?"

Hal was glad the glimmering firelight wouldn't show his flushed cheeks. Lili sat too tensely beside him. Should he move his hand?

"I asked you what sort of wedding you were planning," Esther said.

"Big," Hal said at the same time Lili said, "Small."

Lili cleared her throat. "We haven't talked about it much yet, Bubbe."

"Sure, sure. There's lots of time to talk about that." Esther grinned, her eyes twinkling. In the dim light it was hard to see, but Hal would have bet anything they were the same color as Lili's. "What I really want to know is why you hid this handsome fellow from us for so long."

"Ah, that's been my fault," Hal broke in. "My busy schedule, you know—"

"*Oy vey,* yes," Esther said, nodding. "Doctors, they run themselves ragged, *nu?*"

"Uh—yeah." Hal racked his brain for something, anything, he could say about being a proctologist. "There's certainly a lot of—stuff. To do. A lot of people to—probe. I mean my practice is pretty full."

Esther nodded again, sympathetically. "Lili told me all about it. What a wonderful thing, to be a healer. Now my Saul, he goes to the proctologist. He has these polyps, you see—"

"Bubbe!" Lili coughed. "Hal—oh. Hello! David's on vacation."

"Oh, sure, sorry." Esther waved her hands and sank back into the cushions. "Don't you pay attention to me, David. I'm just an old lady who likes to flap her gums."

"Not at all," Hal said. "I don't mind."

"I like your looks, David." Esther propped her feet up on the low trunk serving as a coffee table between the two couches.

Hal grinned. "Thanks."

"I'd always hoped Lili would find a man with a big nose like the one you've got."

"Bubbe!" Lili cried. She twisted to look at Hal, and he dropped his arm from her shoulder. "His nose isn't big!"

Hal knew he had large features. He'd been told he had a big nose before. Esther's comment didn't hurt his feelings, but he could see that Lili took it personally. For his sake? The thought made warmth flood him.

"Big nose, big hands." Esther craned her neck to peer at Hal's shoes. "*Oy,* and big feet, too!"

"Bubbe!" Lili cried again.

"*Bubbeleh,* don't you know that men with big noses make the best lovers?" Esther asked her granddaughter. "Look at the size of your Zayde Saul's *schnoz!*"

Now Lili was practically writhing in mortification. "Shh. Shh. I don't want to hear any more."

"I ask you," Esther said conversationally to Hal. "How did my son and his wife raise such a prude for a daughter? None of your brothers or sister was this embarrassed when I talked to them."

"It's all right," Hal said, as much for Lili's sake as for Esther's. "Your grandma's right."

Esther hooted. "And such modesty."

He'd just meant she was right about the size of his nose, but he wasn't going to protest the part about being a great lover. "I wish my grandma talked like you do."

"No, you don't," Lili said with a shake of her head. "Bubbe, you're incorrigible."

But now she was smiling and had even relaxed a bit against Hal's side. Lili propped her feet on the table, toying with Esther's boot clad feet playfully. Lili gave the old lady such a look of fondness that, for one instant, Hal was jealous.

"Aunt Lili! David! Come quick!" Noah ran so fast toward him that he skidded on one of the throw rugs on the polished wood floor.

"Whoa, slow down there, buckaroo." Lili caught the boy before he could careen into the furniture. "What's up?"

"It's Henry!" Noah's lip trembled, but at the same time his eyes were alight with excitement. "He was trying to play ping-pong with the big kids and he got hurt! You have to come see!"

Esther leaped to her feet with an agility admirable in an eighty-year-old woman. "Where are they now? Did you tell your mom and dad?"

Noah nodded, full of self-importance at being the messenger. "They said I should go get the doctor."

Hal's heart sank to his ankles and he stifled a groan. He was the doctor. *Still, how bad could a ping-pong injury be?*

Esther had already set off down the hall with Noah tugging at her hand. Hal followed Lili, who moved with a swift, purposeful strides. Her protectiveness of her nieces and nephews was an intriguing look into her character. He'd meant it when he said he thought she'd be a good mother.

"Hurry up!" Noah called back to them before ducking through the doorway to the games lounge. His voice held unmistakable glee. "There's lots of blood!"

Hal stopped dead in the hallway. Lili went a few more steps before seeing he was no longer with her. She came back, frowning.

"Come on," she said. "I want to make sure Henry's okay."

"Blood," Hal said thickly. "Uh—Lili. Er."

"Yes?" She said impatiently, her attention on the cries echoing from just a few feet down the hall.

"Blood." Just saying the word made his stomach churn. "Lili, I can't stand blood."

He saw the memory of their very first meeting register in her eyes. "But they think you're a doctor."

"I'm not a doctor." As if he had to remind her.

The cries grew louder. Lili's consternation grew more visible. It was obvious to him that merely hearing Henry's distress was hurting her.

She could have thrown the fact she was paying him in his face, but she didn't. At this point, Hal doubted if she even remembered that fact. She was too concerned about Henry.

He shook himself mentally and physically. He could do this. He would do this. *For Lili.*

"Doctor Dave to the rescue," he said, and went into the room.

It's only a little blood, he told himself over and over as they found Henry sobbing on his mother's lap. *Gouts and gouts of blood spurting from the little boy's nose.* It had already soaked through someone's thick handkerchief. Hal could see fear in Ruth's eyes, even as she tried to calm her squirming, wailing son.

"David! What should we do?" Frank asked. He hovered over his wife and son, holding Noah's hand.

"It's a bloody nose, so put ice on it," Esther said.

One of the teenage cousins ran for ice. Hal closed his eyes and took a few deep breaths. "Better let me take a look," he said.

Henry stopped crying when he saw Hal. "It hurted my dose," he said in a quavery voice. "And it's buh—buh—bleeding!"

At that admission, Henry started crying again. Ruth, perhaps thinking she was helping, took the bloody cloth away. Hal started seeing gray across the line of his vision.

"Thank God there's a doctor here," said Aunt Yetta, who'd earlier joined them in the hot tub.

Obese Uncle Ira snorted. "He's a proctologist, Yetta. You want he should stick his finger up—"

"Ira!" Yetta scolded.

Ira shrugged and took the bucket of ice from the returning teenager. "Here, doctor."

Hal took the ice and wrapped it in a fresh washcloth someone handed him. He pressed it to the little boy's nose, trying hard not to see the red flowers blooming on the fresh white cloth. *One.* He counted in his mind. *Two. Three—oh, God.* He had to get out of here and fast.

"Hold that there until the bleeding stops," he said in as doctorly a voice as he could. "Tilt his head back and keep the pressure on. And if you'll all excuse me."

Hal stood and left the room. He wasn't running, not quite, but he walked with long, steady strides. Thankfully, the games lounge had a door to the outside and he burst through it. Outside, he gulped in the cool air, trying to settle his stomach. Trying not to think about all the blood.

"You were great in there!" Lili said. "Wow, Hal. You were really, really great."

He wanted, tried, to thank her, but the words were stuck in his throat. Hal closed his eyes, still trying to steady himself. *One. Two. Three.*

"I mean, seeing all that blood," Lili continued, oblivious to his discomfort. "I've never seen one little nose make so much blood."

Every time she said the word, the sight and smell of blood filled his mind. With a groan, Hal relinquished his last shred of self-control. Without a word, he leaned over and threw up on Lili's shoes.

CHAPTER 5

"Are you feeling better?" Lili set the ice bucket down on the bedside table.

Hal nodded, taking away the damp washcloth from over his eyes. Without his glasses on he looked younger, and somehow more vulnerable. Moisture gleamed on his skin.

"I'm sorry," he said.

"If you apologize to me one more time," Lili replied, "I'm going to dump this ice right on your head!"

That coaxed a smile from him. The gesture transformed him. Suddenly, Lili imagined herself pressing her lips to the two tender places at his temples, then lower. To his mouth.

"Put your glasses on!" She blurted, then caught herself. "I mean do you want your glasses?"

"Thanks." Hal slipped them on. "Without them, everything's just one big blur."

Unfortunately, the glasses didn't turn him from Superman back into Clark Kent. *Had he always been so good looking?* How could she not have noticed this before?

Lili busied herself by going into the bathroom to wring out the cloth. When she came out, Hal had swung his legs over the bed. He'd done something to his hair, too, because now it was sticking up all over his head in wild spikes. His stubble stood out clearly on his still-pale cheeks. He'd unbuttoned his shirt and the glimpse of his bare chest and the golden crinkles of hair around his nipples made Lili swallow. Hard.

"Some doctor I'm turning out to be," Hal said with just a trace of mockery in his voice.

"To be fair, you are a proctologist. They probably don't have to deal with a lot of blood." Lili couldn't help smiling at Hal's squeamish expression.

"I just hope everyone else around here remains accident free." Hal buttoned his shirt and smoothed his hair, becoming once again the man she'd hired instead of some lust-inspiring dreamboat. Lili realized she preferred him disheveled.

"At least nobody noticed you got sick," Lili pointed out helpfully.

Hal shrugged. "So I didn't blow your cover."

That wasn't what she'd meant actually. She'd been thinking more that he wouldn't have to be embarrassed. It was, however, just one more reminder she had paid for Hal to act as her fiancé. It was a fact she inconveniently kept forgetting.

"Do you feel up to heading out again?" She checked her watch. "It's going to be dinner time soon."

She heard his stomach rumble even from where she stood.

"I'll take that as a yes."

Hal stood and stretched. "I feel fine now. What's on the agenda for tonight?"

Lili had to pass him to get to the printed sheet listing both Bramblewood's planned activities and the Alster family week's activities. With the bed just behind him, Hal had no room to get out of the way. When she brushed his chest with her shoulder, Lili's entire arm tingled.

She made it to the dresser at the foot of the bed and snatched up the paper. "Looks like the resort had several hikes planned for the afternoon, but we missed most of them. More games in the lounge. In about twenty minutes, they're going to show *The Bridges of Madison County* in the TV lounge. They have a caricaturist set up in the main lounge from four to five, and at five o'clock, there's a happy hour special." She flipped the sheet over. "Six pm we have dinner in the reserved dining room with the family. Anything sound appealing?"

She glanced up into the mirror over the dresser as she spoke. Only the fact she'd already finished speaking kept the words from drying in her throat. She'd caught Hal staring at her. There was no mistaking the desire in his eyes, and when he saw she was looking, he quickly looked away.

"Whatever you'd like to do is fine with me."

Oh, she could think of several things she wanted to do. None of them involved leaving this room. Lili took a deep breath and forced herself to think rationally. Her family might be expecting her and Hal to be sequestered in their room and knocking boots all day and night, but the reality of the situation was that they barely knew each other.

"We could just take a walk around the grounds," Lili said. "It's a beautiful resort."

"Okay."

"We—we might run into my family all over the place."

He nodded. "That's okay, too. We're here to spend time with them, right?"

"Right." She took another deep breath. "You ready?"

He stepped aside so she could lead the way out the door. The sun dipped low in the sky, and the air was fresh and crisp. Lili raised her face to the breeze, willing it to whisk away all the crazy feelings she'd been having. Lili reflected that a simple fall breeze wouldn't be enough. She'd probably need a hurricane.

Hal took her hand as they walked, almost as naturally as if they truly were a couple. "Hey, guys!" Ruth called to them from a short distance. "Where'd you disappear to?"

"We were a little tired, so we headed back to the room for a nap." The lie slipped out so easily that Lili felt guilty.

Ruth smiled and winked. "Sure you did."

Hal put his arm around Lili and bent to nuzzle her cheek. "Sure, we did."

Ruth laughed. "You crazy kids. Oh, to be young and in love again."

"You talk like you and Frank are old farts sitting around knitting socks," Lili said. Ruth was only three years older than she.

"Honey," Ruth said in a forced, thick, New York accent. "When youse've been married as long as me and Frank, getting a little action means getting the kids to bed early so you can fall asleep watching television together."

Hal put up his hands in mock fear. "Ruth, you're scaring me off. Lili's just about convinced me that walking down the aisle is the greatest thing since sliced bread. Don't ruin it!"

Lili glanced at him shrewdly. *Just about convinced him?* Hal was good, really good. He was setting things up nicely for a break up.

"Yeah, Ruth," Lili chimed in. "Don't talk like that to Mr. Commitment-Is-A-Dirty-Word here."

Hal laughed a little too hard. "C'mon, Lil. You know I've always said that in order to be committed, you have to be insane!"

Now Ruth looked uneasily at them. Lili knew she'd better ease off. She didn't want to ruin Bubbe and Zayde's celebration, which meant the break up couldn't happen until just before the week ended. They still had to get through four more days.

"Oh, David," Lili said with as much forced joviality as she could muster. She punched his arm playfully. "You're such a joker."

She was proud of the way he caught on. "Oh, Lil. You know I'm insane. Insane for you!"

He lifted her in the air and twirled her around, smacking kisses on her cheek that made her giggle. When he put her down, Ruth just shook her head at them.

"Anyway, thanks for your help with Henry earlier. He's so accident-prone, it's a wonder I don't have a head of gray hair." Ruth smoothed her dark hair back from her forehead.

"Any time," Hal answered smoothly. "I hope he's doing okay."

Ruth paused before answering to point into the distance. Henry ran after Noah, who in turn chased one of the girl cousins. The children ran around and around the baseball field, sending their laughing shouts through the crisp fall air.

"I'd say he's doing fine," Ruth said wryly. "And I'm off to get a massage."

Lili oohed. "That sounds nice!"

"Lots of us are getting one. You should get one, too!" Ruth rolled her head on her shoulders, wincing. "They come right to your room and do it."

Lili thought of her already rapidly depleting bank account and shrugged. Even with Ian's insurance money, this trip was costing a fortune. "Maybe some other time. It's pretty expensive."

"Then just get your man there to give you one," Ruth said, setting off. "He looks like he'd be pretty good at it!"

When Ruth had passed out of hearing range, Hal said, "I could give you a massage, if you want."

"Hal, that's not part of the package." Lili headed toward the small bridge spanning a chuckling stream. In the summer time, there'd be ducks. Today only the water rippled through the grass.

"No, I mean it." Hal followed her over the charming log bridge and along the trail through a small patch of woods. "A real massage. That's what I'm going to school for."

That stopped her. "Really? But your resumé said you had degrees in business and accounting."

A cloud passed over his face. "I don't do that any more."

The trail was still clear of leaves, most of which still clung to the trees in brilliant shades of orange, red and gold. It wouldn't be long before they fell and left the trees bare and the path covered , but for now Lili walked with Hal and felt as though they might be the only two people around for miles.

"Why not?" she asked eventually, when several minutes had passed with only the sound of their feet crunching on the gravel.

"I had my own business. Kessler, Kessler and Bower." Lili heard a note of bitter pride in Hal's voice. "We were voted most successful new business our first year out. We did really well for five years."

"And then?" Lili prompted.

Hal's smile was forced. "Kessler and Bower ran off to the Bahamas and filed for divorce, taking two-thirds of the business with them."

Somehow Lili didn't see Hal running away to the Bahamas. "Your wife?"

"Ex-wife," he corrected. "And ex-partner. John and I had known each other for fifteen years."

"Ouch." Lili pulled her coat closer around her neck. "Hal, that's terrible. I'm sorry."

"Yeah, me, too." He kicked a pile of leaves that had accumulated. "To make it worse, they sued me for my third of the practice. They won."

"And that's why you're working for LoveMatch." Suddenly it all clicked together. "But you're going to school, too?"

"Massage Therapy and Healing Touch." Hal stretched out his hands and wiggled the fingers. "I figured that making people feel better made more sense than just making them feel richer."

"I'm impressed."

He looked sideways at her. "Yeah?"

Lili nodded and slipped her hand into his, even though there was nobody around to see them. "Yeah."

*   *   *

Once again, dinner was riotous. It was a good thing the Alsters had reserved the private dining room for the entire week. Hal couldn't imagine this group eating with the rest of Bramblewood's guests. Dessert was only now being served and the clock said nearly eight o'clock.

He and Lili were seated across from each other. Every so often she'd break off whatever she was doing and look at him. Hal was always looking back.

"Can't you take your eyes off him for just one second and talk to your own mother?" Lili's mother Irene teased her daughter.

Lili blushed. "Oh, Ma."

Irene gave Lili a squeeze around the shoulders. "Don't worry about it, doll. He's a catch."

Seeing them so close together, Hal saw how much Lili resembled her mother. They both had the same sleek, dark hair, though Irene's was shot through with strands of silver. The same mouth and chin. It was easy to see what Lili would look like in thirty years or so. Hal wished he'd have the opportunity.

"It's such a shame you had to leave the ring at the jeweler's to be refitted," Irene went on. She grabbed up Lili's hand and rubbed the bare finger. "It just doesn't seem the same without a ring on the finger."

"No, it sure doesn't," Lili said with a glance at Hal.

Remembering earlier how Lili had injected conflict into the conversation to set up the break up, Hal thought this might be a good time to do a little more. "If Lili didn't have such fat fingers, the ring would've fit perfectly."

Lili's light expression turned fierce. "Fat fingers?"

Irene clucked, patting Lili's hand. "Dear, I'm sure David didn't mean it the way it sounded."

"Sure I did," Hal said cheerfully. "They're like little sausages. Plump, little sausages."

Lili snatched her hand out of her mother's grip and looked at it, her expression appalled. "They are not!"

"Lili, I think David's teasing you." Irene frowned. "At least, I hope he's teasing."

Hal leaned across as though he had a secret to tell Irene. "I keep telling her she'd better quit eating so much or she's never going to fit into her wedding dress." He laughed at his own witticism. "I mean, just because we're going on a honeymoon cruise is no excuse to start looking like a whale!"

Now Irene's frown deepened. She looked at Lili's scowling face and back to Hal. "David, Lili has a beautiful figure. How can you say she's fat?"

"Oh, it's all right, Mrs. Alster. Lili knows I like my women plump. Makes it easier to catch 'em when they try to run away!"

"And I can't imagine why they'd try," Irene said dryly. She kissed

Lili's cheek. "I'm going to talk to your bubbe, Lili. We'll see you later?"

Lili's reply was terse. "Yes. I think so."

"Good." Irene patted Lili's shoulder, gave Hal a dubious glance, and left her seat.

When the server placed Lili's thick slice of chocolate cake in front of her, she didn't pick up her fork to eat. Hal dove into his and demolished it in several bites. Curiously, he watched as Lili just sat and stared.

"Aren't you going to eat that?" he asked. Silently, she shook her head no. "Mind if I have it?"

Again, she didn't speak, but indicated with her hand that he was to go ahead. He did. It was delicious.

"Ahhh." He sighed, patting his stomach, which would definitely suffer for this week's indulgences. He'd have to hit the gym pretty hard for the next month. "That was great."

"Glad you enjoyed it." In the midst of the chaos broiling all around them, Lili's answer was dangerously soft. In fact, he almost missed it.

Lili's brother, Eli, slipped into the chair her mother had vacated. "Thanks again for your help this afternoon with Henry. He's always getting banged up."

"Better than getting knocked up, right, Lil?" Hal reached across the table to poke her arm good-humoredly. He was beginning to enjoy playing the role Lili had assigned him. He'd always wanted to try out for a part in a play.

"David," Lili said through gritted teeth. Her smile was strained. "I don't think—"

"Lili?" Elijah had turned to look at her, brow furrowed. "You okay?"

"Fine," Lili answered.

Her brother didn't seem convinced.

"Hey, you know women," Hal said. "Always got a bug up their bloomers about something."

Eli just stared at him before nodding slowly. He gave his sister another thoughtful glance. "Yeah. Whatever. Lili?"

"I'm fine," she told him. "Just tired. I think I'll head back to the room early."

"Great idea!" Hal said. He pushed back from the table. "You know you could always use some extra beauty sleep. I mean, hey, I could pack my wardrobe in the bags under your eyes—"

Lili shot him a look so murderous Hal took a step back. "Good night, Eli," she said and got up from the table. She left the room quickly, leaving Hal to stand behind and stare after her.

"Oops," Hal said, but without enthusiasm. He'd screwed up. He wasn't sure quite how, but he knew he had.

"I'd say so," Eli said with a shake of his head. "You'll be sleeping on the couch tonight."

He already had to sleep on the couch, but Eli didn't know that. "Yeah. I guess I'd better go see about her."

Eli merely raised his eyebrows and shrugged. "I'd let her cool off for a while, but I guess you know her well enough to decide for yourself."

"Yeah," Hal replied weakly.

The problem was, he didn't know Lili at all.

*   *   *

Lili worked her numb fingers around the old-fashioned radiator knob to no avail. It was stuck solid. The metal bars were only lukewarm, not hot enough to combat the night's sudden bitter dip to temperatures. She tried again, cursing under her breath as her fingers slipped, and she scraped her knuckles.

The knock on the door made her whirl around, fuming. *Hal?* Unless he had a wrench with him or a container of hot coffee, she wasn't much interested in seeing him. The knock came again. Rap, rap, rap.

"Who is it?" Lili hollered.

His answer was muffled. "It's me. David."

At least he wasn't having any trouble staying in character. If she'd had any doubts, their conversation at dinner tonight had proved that! Lili crossed the room, skirting the bed and the pile of blankets on the couch.

She flung open the door and turned immediately around, refusing to look at him. "Shut the door. It's freezing out there!"

"In here, too."

She heard him stomping his feet and blowing into his hands.

"That's not going to help this radiator," she said, still trying to work the controls.

"Have you called housekeeping?" Hal asked.

He came up behind her, close. Too close. Lili stiffened, silently warning him to keep his distance. He backed off a step.

"Of course I've called housekeeping," she said coldly. "Unfortunately, their night service man called in drunk tonight."

"Did you tell them how cold it was in here?" Hal's chattering teeth interrupted his calm question.

Still angry with him for his boorish behavior at dinner, Lili whirled on him. "No, Mr. Smartypants! I didn't! You know why? Because there aren't any other rooms available. The inn's all booked up, and I didn't want to ruin my grandparent's week by complaining about something that could easily be fixed in the morning!"

Hal held up his hands. "Whoa. Okay."

Lili blew hard, gusting the hank of hair off her forehead. "The knob is stuck."

"Can I take a look?"

Lili stepped aside. "Be my guest."

Hal pondered the radiator's configuration, running his large hands over the metal. He tried twisting it. He tried pushing it. With every failed effort, Lili could see him becoming more and more determined. It was that male ego thing.

"If I just yank on it hard enough," Hal said, grunting.

Lili leaned in for a closer look. "It's not going to budge."

"I can get it," Hal insisted. He put one foot up to brace himself, then put both hands on the slippery metal knob.

Lili bent down to peer under his arms. "You'll never get it."

"I'll get it!"

Hal puffed and groaned, tugging. He was really putting a lot of force into it. If Lili hadn't still been so miffed about his earlier performance at dinner, she might even have admired his strength.

The knob suddenly let go. Hal's arms flew backward, his elbow catching Lili square in her right eye. The force of the blow knocked her to her knees, too stunned to even cry out. Hal tottered on unbalanced legs for one moment before tripping over her prone body. He landed right on her, crushing the air out of her in a strangled wheeze.

Lili would have yelled if she'd been able to breathe. As it was, the blow to her eye had temporarily blinded her to anything but flashing red spots. Without breath in her lungs, all she could do was gasp and claw at the carpet.

"Lili! Are you okay?" Hal rolled off her, and gathered her into his arms.

Lili still couldn't speak, though her vision was returning slowly. She felt like an elephant had sat on her. She must have looked as awful as she felt because Hal scooped her up and staggered with her toward the tiny bathroom.

From her one good eye, every bit of detritus and debris scattered on the floor became magnified a million times. *No!* Her mind screamed, watching Hal's big foot connect with a particularly messy tangle of his socks. *No!*

But he caught himself, saving them both from hitting the floor again with a heroic effort. The next thing she knew, Lili was sitting on the toilet seat. Hal ran cold water on the washcloth hanging in the tub and pressed it to her eye. The shock of it made her gasp again. When she pulled the white cloth away, it was tinged pink.

"You must have clipped your head on the edge of the bed," Hal said. He gently took the cloth from her and pressed it back to the wound, which was starting to sting. "Oh, Lili, I'm so sorry."

"You say that a lot," Lili managed to reply.

She didn't mean to cry, but all at once the tears came slipping down her cheeks in fat, hot tracks. The sobs wrenched out of her chest, hurting her sore ribs. It was more than embarrassing, the way she burst loose, but Lili couldn't stop it any more than she could have stopped Hal from knocking her over.

He smells so nice, she thought blearily, as he pulled her against his chest. *Like fresh air. Like mint.*

His arms around her were strong and warm. His hand stroked her hair in long, gentle sweeps that made her scalp tingle. Being hugged by Hal was wonderfully comforting. Strangely, all of that made her cry harder.

Hal murmured her name, tugging her down off her perch and into his lap. He tucked her head neatly under the curve of his chin, settling her more firmly into his embrace. With smooth, gentle movements he rocked her, all the while just holding her and stroking her hair.

"I'm so sorry," he whispered again. "Oh, Lili, believe me. I'm a big, dumb klutz, but I'd never, ever, want to hurt you."

"Then why did you say I'm f—f—fat?" The last word wailed out of her. Lili's sobs regenerated.

The rocking paused for just a moment. "What?"

She pulled away from him to look him in the face. "At dinner! You said I had fat fingers and b—bags under my eyes!"

Hal frowned. "I was just trying to be an insensitive jerk."

"Well, you succeeded!"

Now her sobs tapered off into just a few, chest-hitching sniffles. Lili's face felt hot, her eye swollen, her nose a runny, sloppy mess. Hal reached across her to the toilet paper roll and pulled off a thick handful of paper.

Lili blew her nose messily and wiped her eyes. "Ouch!"

Hal handed her the still cool cloth. "Put this on. We'll get some ice for it. You're going to have a real shiner, though."

She dabbed at her eye, feeling the sore spot just above her brow. The cloth came back even pinker. Lili groaned, pressing it back against the ache.

Hal shifted a little, easing her off his thighs. "My legs are falling asleep."

Lili realized they were sitting squashed between the clawfoot tub and the pedestal sink. Hal had drawn his long legs into a criss-cross in order to hold her on his lap, and his head pressed precariously against the sink's underside. Her own back rubbed uncomfortably against the overhanging lip on the tub. The tile floor was cold, too.

Awkwardly, they disentangled themselves. Lili got up. Again the red spots flashed in front of her eyes and she had to grab the sink to keep from falling. Hal held her hand, helping her back to her prior seat on the toilet.

"I only said those things because I thought you'd want me to," Hal told her.

Lili felt recovered enough to try sarcasm. "Sure. What woman doesn't like being told she's fat and has bags under her eyes?"

Hal looked perplexed. "Women don't like that."

"Duh!" Lili scowled. "So what made you think I would?"

Hal sighed. "I didn't think you would. I just thought the whole point was we were going to break up. I was just giving you reasons."

"You did a good job," Lili replied.

She noticed he was still holding her hand. Her anger started to slip away, and now she could step back and look at the situation in a different light. Of course Hal was trying to be a jerk. That's what she'd paid him to do.

"If it helps," he said almost shyly, "I didn't mean any of those things."

"No?" Lili took the cloth away again with a little hiss of pain. A red flower had blossomed in the center of the fabric, but the bleeding appeared to have stopped.

"Of course not." Hal cleared his throat. "Lili, I think you are one of the most beautiful women I've ever dated."

That stopped her completely. "You do?"

He smiled, the unexpectedly sexy smile that made her toes curl.

"Sure."

"Well." Lili didn't have much else to say. His words made her feel incredibly warm all over, and she had to bite her lip to keep from giggling like a giddy schoolgirl. "Thanks."

Hal seemed warm too. His face was flushed and bright beads of sweat were gathering on his forehead. Lili's cheeks felt uncomfortably hot, too, even for a blush. Then she noticed it was more than just her cheeks that felt warm. Her entire body was beginning to sweat.

"Is it hot in here?" she asked.

Hal nodded, unzipping his fleece jacket. "Yeah. Really warm."

"The radiator!" They both spoke at the same time.

Near-tropical heat greeted them when they went back into the bedroom. The radiator, which before had stubbornly refused to let out more than an early spring day's worth of temperature had now gone straight to an August heat wave. The windows and mirror over the dresser had steamed over.

"I guess you fixed it," Lili said.

Hal took off his coat and hung it on the hook behind the door. "It's like an oven in here!"

"I'll open a window," Lili said, but when she tried to cross the room to do so, she felt so light-headed she had to sit down on the bed.

"I'll do it." Hal slid the window open a crack, letting in a blast of blessedly frigid air. He sighed, sticking his face into the breeze. "That's better!"

"If you moved out of the way," Lili said crossly, "I might be able to get some, too!"

Hal gave her a sheepish grin and moved. "Better?"

She nodded, swallowing. Her head was beginning to throb terribly. The cloth was no longer cool, and no longer very damp.

"Let me see." The bed sank as Hal sat down next to her, taking the cloth away. "It looks better. Do you want some ice to put on it?"

"I think we need some ice," Lili said. "Not just for my eye either."

"I'll get some." Hal took her hand and helped her scoot back on the bed. "You lie down here. I'll take care of it."

It's nice, Lili reflected, *being pampered.* Hal turned the small television on, brought her aspirin and some cool water from the bathroom, and even plumped her pillows. He refreshed the damp cloth and helped her take off her shoes.

"I'll be right back," he said.

After he'd gone, Lili took the washcloth off her eye and probed the tender spot. It was going to be sore for a while, but the aspirin had started to kick in. She laid the pink-tinged cloth on the bedside table, then realized something weird. Something interesting, that made her feel even warmer than the room's tropic temperatures.

She'd been bleeding, but Hal hadn't noticed.

CHAPTER 6

Spending the night sweating and writhing around on his bed would have been fun, except, of course, that he'd done it alone. Hal sluiced cool water over himself, rinsing away the night's stickiness. Sleeping in the room had been like sleeping in a sauna.

He really wanted a shower, not a half-hearted soak in the claw-foot tub. Something brisk and refreshing to wake him up. He hadn't slept well. Between the heat and the erotic dreams he'd kept having about Lili, the hard and lumpy loveseat had seemed even more uncomfortable.

"Are you almost finished?" Lili rapped on the closed door. "I'm starving!"

"I'll be right out." Hal stepped out of the tub and toweled off. He brushed his teeth and ran his fingers through his hair, then opened the door.

Lili tapped the off button on the remote and laid it on top of the television. In the morning light, her eye looked even more horrific than it had the night before. Added to the swelled eye and cut brow were assorted other bruises on her cheek and forehead. He'd really nailed her.

She hadn't bothered trying to conceal the wounds with makeup either. Hal admired that. He knew her face would raise a lot of questions, but if Lili was willing to face them, so was he.

"Another day in the Alster family week of torture!" she intoned lightly. "Prepare yourself for another day of hiking, arts and crafts, and general merriment!"

"It hasn't been that bad," Hal said, watching her smile. He could watch her for hours.

"Not yet." Lili raised her uninjured brow. "There's still time."

"Starting with breakfast," Hal said.

She groaned, holding her stomach. "It's all too much!"

"Your family really isn't that bad," Hal told her.

Lili laughed. "I meant too much food, Hal. But thanks. They just haven't started the real grilling yet. Give them time."

Though the room was still stifling, the air outside was chill. Gray clouds hung low in the sky. Lili shivered as she stepped out and Hal joined her. It was more than just cold out here; it was downright bitter.

"I'm glad there's no ride scheduled for today," Lili remarked as they set off on the now-familiar path toward the main lodge. "I think I'm just going to stick by the fire."

That sounded good to Hal, too. *Prop my feet up, read a good book. Lili would rest her head on my shoulder, and—* Whoa, he was getting carried away. Hal fought off the daydream. There was no sense in thinking about things that would only be fake if they happened at all.

"'Morning!" Lili called to the table reserved for her family.

Hal braced himself for the comments on Lili's bruises, but none came. The table fell silent as they approached it. The subdued air was vastly different from the previous meals the family had shared.

Hal saw Lili's mother and Bubbe share a look as he and Lili sat down, but neither said anything. In fact, nobody said anything at all until little Henry spoke up.

"Gee, Aunt Lili," he said with syrup-smeared lips. "What happened to your face?"

"Henry!" Ruth snapped. "Don't bother Aunt Lili."

Lili's hand flew up to touch her eye. "I tripped," she said cheerfully, sliding into the chair next to Henry's. "Pretty clumsy, huh?"

"Did Dr. Dave help you with your eye like he helped me with my nose?" Henry asked solemnly, chewing on another mouthful of pancake.

Lili gave Hal a smile. "He sure did."

"I'll bet he did," Hal heard Eli mutter. Lili's brother got up from the table and tossed down his napkin. "I think I'm done. Sarah?"

Eli's wife gathered their three daughters and hiked their infant son up onto her hip. Hal couldn't be imagining the scowl she gave him. She looked like she wanted to slap him.

Ruth squeezed Lili's shoulder as she stood. "Let's talk," she stage-whispered.

"Okay," Lili said, her tone bewildered.

"Later," Ruth said with a glance at Hal that had his heart settling into his mismatched socks.

The table cleared quickly after that, with every one of Lili's relatives giving her sympathetic looks and scowling at Hal. Finally, they were the only two left at the table. Lili sat back in her chair with a bemused laugh.

"Do we smell bad?" she asked.

Hal took a listless sip of his orange juice. "I think they're mad at me."

"Already?" Lili hooted. "Damn, Hal, you're good. What did you do?"

"Well for starters," he said glumly, "I beat you."

"You…" Lili touched her face again. "Oh, I'm sure they don't think that."

He thought of the looks her family had given him. "Want to bet?"

She looked disturbed. "I want them to be happy I'm not going to marry you, not think you're evil."

He shrugged. "Did you look in the mirror today?"

"As little as possible." Lili curled her fingers over her his for just a moment. "Don't worry, Hal. It'll be okay."

"If you say so," Hal replied, but he didn't believe her.

*　　　*　　　*

As was the norm for Alster vacations, every spare moment of the day was crammed with things to do. Though they'd been abandoned at breakfast, Lili and Hal found themselves converged upon and dragged into every conceivable activity as the day went on.

First it was the Wang Dang Doodle Tango contest held in the games lounge. Complete with wacky DJ and themed decorations, the game attracted most of the resort's younger population.

So much for my quiet afternoon by the fire, Lili thought with a wince as the music screeched even louder.

After the tango contest, which neither she nor Hal managed to finish, Lili's mother insisted the two of them go with her to the crafts room to make pinecone bird feeders. Aside from the resort counselors, the three of them were the room's only adult occupants.

"It's just precious," Irene said, dangling Lili's glittery, peanut-buttery creation from its yarn loop. "You can hang it from a tree in your yard!"

"Mom," Lili said impatiently. "I don't have a backyard. I live in a townhouse."

"Whatever," Irene said airily, in a way that made Lili suspicious.

What exactly was going on? Had her family gone even nuttier than usual? Lili watched Hal fight with his pinecone. The peanut butter got all over his fingers, which he then promptly burned with the hot glue gun.

"I think we're done," Lili said wryly to the counselor who came over to check their progress.

"Good," said Irene firmly. She tugged Lili from the table, but ignored the struggling Hal. "Because it's time for the makeovers."

"Makeovers?" Lili stopped, resisting her mother's tugging. "What makeovers?"

"Bubbe scheduled them for all of us ladies," Irene said with a glance at Hal. "David will have to find something else to do."

"You go ahead, Lili," Hal said. He bit his lip in concentration, forcing the thin strand of yarn into a loop. It slipped from his fingers and he grabbed it angrily. "I want to finish this."

Had there ever been a more adorable man? Lili thought fondly, watching his efforts. Hal really was a nice guy. How a man could look sexy with a pinecone between his knees and peanut butter on his hands, Lili didn't know. But Hal did.

It wasn't until her mother locked the door to the ladies' spa room behind them that Lili began suspecting something more than just unusual nuttiness. Just as at breakfast, the room fell silent when she entered. Her sister, her mother, Bubbe, even her aunts and cousins just stared at her.

"What?" Lili asked.

"It's going to take a lot of makeup to cover up that," Bubbe said aloud.

Lili's laugh was forced. "This? It's nothing. Just a little bruise."

Bubbe snorted and shot a look at Irene. Lili didn't miss the silent communication, but she wasn't sure what it meant. Ruth snorted, too, in a perfect copy of Bubbe's, and Lili sighed in exasperation.

"Please," she said. "I'm fine!"

The woman dressed all in white cleared her throat uncomfortably. "Ladies? Are we ready?"

Bubbe flapped her hands and cast a dire glance at Lili. "Yes, Vera, let's get started already."

Getting started turned out to mean slathering gobs of white, noxious smelling cream all over their faces. Lili breathed through her mouth and tried to ignore the sting of the stuff against her scraped eyebrow. Slowly, the natural propensity of her female relatives to gossip and chatter overcame whatever had kept them silent before.

"Now, ladies," said Vera, holding up a small plate covered with more gobs of stuff. "Let's get started on the foundation."

"You know you can always talk to me about anything," Ruth whispered as she and Lili scrubbed their faces clean of the white cream.

"Sure, Ruthie, I know." Lili was startled when Ruth laid her hand on Lili's. Seeing Ruth's concerned look, Lili smiled to ease her mind. "I know."

"I know you know," Ruth said. She took a small jar of Vera's foundation. "But would you? Talk to me?"

"Sure I would," Lili said. She took a pot for herself. "If I had anything to talk about, which I don't."

Ruth sighed, dipping her finger into the goo and spreading it on her cheeks. "Just so you know I'm always here for you. That's all. If you need advice, or to talk. Are you sure you don't have something you need to tell me? Something—impending?"

Lili was touched by her sister's offer. "Thanks, Ruthie. But I'm fine. Really."

Ruth reached out and lightly brushed her fingers across Lili's brow. "That doesn't look fine."

So Hal was right. They did think he had beaten her. Lili thought of her last night with Ian, and the way he'd treated her. Nobody knew the truth about him, their relationship, or what had happened. Lili grabbed Ruth's hand and impulsively kissed her sister's fingers before pushing them away.

"I tripped. You act like H—David hit me or something."

Ruth didn't smile even though Lili had. "Didn't he?"

Lili rolled her eyes. "Of course not."

He'd just slammed his elbow into her eye, knocked her over, then landed on her. *But that all had been an accident!* Lili thought of the way he'd taken care of her afterwards, and couldn't stop a dreamy smile from painting itself on her lips.

Ruth lowered her voice, keeping their conversation to the small table they shared. "That's some bunch of bruises from just tripping."

Lili's smile faded. "I told you I'm fine."

Ruth peered into her mirror, globbing on the thick foundation as

Vera lectured from the front of the room on how to apply the goop. "I'm just saying, that's all."

"Don't you believe me?" Lili asked, her voice a little loud. She saw her mother and Bubbe exchanging another of their looks, and she lowered her voice. "Ruth?"

Ruth paused in her smudging and feathering to look squarely at her. "Should I?"

"Yes!" Lili said adamantly.

Ruth stared for one intense moment before bending back to her makeup. Lili fumed. Why shouldn't her sister believe her? A guilty thought struck her. Unless she'd spent so much time lying to her family already that now even the truth had become unbelievable.

*   *   *

Lili's family had spent the entire day inventing reasons for them to be apart. Lili wasn't joking when she told him the grilling hadn't yet begun either. While the women whisked Lili off to makeovers, spa visits and aerobics classes, the men pounded Hal for answers.

What he hated most was the loathing in Eli's eyes when he cornered Hal.

"I love my sister," he said. "And I hope you don't think I'm going to let anything, or anybody, hurt her."

Hal had mumbled some sort of reply—one that didn't seem to impress Eli. Then he'd escaped back to the blistering room and holed up there until dinner. At least he'd been able to get the front desk to send someone to fix the radiator, so the room should be a comfortable temperature by bedtime.

They ate dinner again in the separate dining room. It was just as active and loud as the past nights had been, though this time Hal noticed everybody was ignoring him. He comforted himself with the thought that this was exactly what Lili wanted. Heck, if things kept going this way, they wouldn't even have to break up. Her family would run him out of town on a rail.

"You didn't eat very much," Lili said as they left the dining room.

While every one else was heading out for an evening dip in the pool or for other planned events, all Hal wanted to do was go back to the room. The thought of facing another firing line of stares and scowls was beginning to wear on him.

"Like you said, it's all too much."

They paused on the front porch. The temperature had dropped even further, and plumes of frosty air came out of their mouths with every breath. Hal snuck a glance at the porch swing where Lili had kissed him so passionately. *Was it only last night?*

"Look at those stars," Lili murmured from beside him.

From the door behind them they heard the bustle of people coming outside. Instantly, they reached for each other's hands. Lili chuckled softly when a group of resort guests unrelated to her passed them by.

"Habit," she said, as though in apology, but she didn't drop his hand.

The stars she'd mentioned were like bright diamonds set against a rippling curtain of black velvet. Even with the air so frigid, it was a sight to move even the least romantic of souls. It was a night made for snuggling under blankets and drinking cocoa. A night for making love in front of a roaring fire.

"Hey, look at that!" Lili pointed toward the front of the house, to the large circular driveway. "Carriage rides!"

"I don't suppose they'll have many takers tonight," Hal said.

Lili turned to look at him, mischief dancing in her eyes. "Let's go!"

"Now?"

"Yes, now," she teased. "Of course, now. Why not?"

"You want to go on a carriage ride with me?" Hal had to ask.

Lili pursed her lips. "Well, yeah. That's sort of the point, Hal."

He nodded firmly, feeling suddenly better than he had all day. "All right, then!"

Just as they reached the carriage, Frank and Ruth appeared out of the night. "There you are," Ruth said. "We've been looking for you all over."

"If you want to drag us into some lame game again, forget it," Lili said, though with good humor.

"Bubbe's arranged a karaoke party," Ruth said. "Come on. It's going to be hilarious."

"Have a good time," Lili said, and motioned for Hal to get into the carriage. She climbed up beside him. "We're going to take a carriage ride."

"I really think you should come with us," Ruth said. "Lili?"

"Nope, sorry," Lili said. She laughed. "All of you have been working hard all day at keeping me and H—honeybuns apart. Now we're going to take a carriage ride. Alone."

"But we really want—" Ruth began, but Lili tapped the driver's shoulder to urge him on.

"Later," Lili called.

The carriage pulled away, the wheels crunching on the gravel path it followed into the meadow. The driver asked them how long a ride they wanted, and seemed pleased when Lili replied as long as he wanted to drive, they'd be willing to ride. After that, it was as though they were alone in the carriage under the stars.

"Honeybuns?" Hal said finally.

Lili tugged the plaid blanket more firmly across their knees. "I had to think of something, quick. You know what I almost said."

"Honeybuns." Hal grinned. "I like it."

Lili punched his arm gently. "You'd better. I'm going to have to call you that from now on."

"I've been called worse."

Lili sighed, settling back against the seat. The carriage was small, just large enough for two people with the driver in front. With every movement of the horses, Hal and Lili rubbed against each other. Hal found he didn't mind that at all.

"It's so beautiful out here," Lili said wistfully, staring up into the night sky. "I wish I didn't have to go back."

"Back to Bramblewood? Or back to work?" Hal asked. The carriage hit a bump, rocking them together. He slipped his arm around her shoulders to help cushion her from future rough terrain.

"Both." Lili snuggled down further against him, deeper into the blankets.

"Me, too."

She squirmed around until she could look up at him. In the starlight, her eyes were luminous. "You mean you're not all excited about heading back to LoveMatch?"

Hal blew out a gust of air that steamed his glasses. "Yeah, right. I'm so successful at it."

Lili nudged him. "I think you're pretty successful at it."

Hal drew her in closer. "Lili, I'm glad you…" He paused, aware of the driver, who, though silent, must still be listening to every word. "I'm glad you chose me as your fiancé."

The wording was benign enough nobody could possibly guess that their pairing had been a financial and not a romantic one. Lili seemed to understand his careful sentence. She nodded, then rested her head on his shoulder.

"Me, too," she said.

They rode like that for a few more minutes, and the carriage finally returned to the driveway. "Thanks, folks," said the driver.

Hal helped Lili down, and for just a moment, her body pressed against his as she stepped from the carriage. It was the perfect moment for a kiss. A real kiss this time. And to Hal's surprise, because things with him always had a way of going wrong, Lili met his mouth at the same time he bent to kiss her.

They didn't clash teeth. There was no bloodshed. He didn't even step on her feet. Instead, there was just the sweet pressure of her lips on his, the faint smell of roses in the crisp fall hair, and the feeling of Lili's dark hair tickling his cheek.

For once, Hal had done something right.

*   *   *

"They fixed the radiator." It was the first thing Lili noticed when she walked in the room. Replacing the sweltering temperature of earlier was a chill burst of air nearly equaling that from outside. She couldn't quite see her breath—quite.

"This afternoon." Hal stumbled over something on the floor, holding out his hands for balance. His glasses were steamed up.

Lili grabbed his hand to help him. "Don't fall. We don't want my family thinking that I'm beating you."

He only smiled at the joke she'd hoped might earn a laugh. Apparently he was really bothered everyone seemed to believe he hit her. Truthfully, it bothered Lili, too, but the thought of Hal raising a hand to her in anger was ridiculous.

"It's late," he said. "I guess we'd better get ready for bed."

Lili felt a little light-headed at the thought and she didn't even have the excuse of an overheated room to blame it on. The kiss they'd just shared had been sweet, but with undercurrents of passion she wasn't sure she was ready to explore. Or, for that matter, certain she could ignore.

"Another early morning tomorrow," she replied with forced lightness. She yawned and stretched, also forced.

Neither one of them moved. Hal took a halting step toward her, then snatched off his glasses and swiped them furiously with his shirt tail to clear them. Lili was in a fever of anticipation. He was going to kiss her again. Did she want him to? Could she stand it if he didn't?

The phone rang, startling both of them. Hal, who was closer, went to the jangling box and lifted the receiver. Lili's heart began beating again. She hadn't realized it had stopped.

"No, not really. Tomorrow morning? Okay." He hung up, turning to her. "Front desk wanting to be sure the radiator was fixed."

They stood where they were, but the hesitant mood had been broken. Lili lifted her chin, pretending she wasn't disappointed. *It was just as well, really.* There was no use in creating awkward entanglements.

By unspoken agreement, she used the bathroom first. As she brushed her teeth, her mouth filled with suds, she thought it was just one more thing in a very long list about Hal she was growing to like. He was considerate.

Lili washed her face carefully, scrubbing away the last remnants of the afternoon's makeover. She ran steaming hot water in the tub and washed herself. She even shaved her legs, telling herself it was only because she couldn't stand the stubble rubbing against her flannel nightie.

Finally, there were no more ablutions, no more preparations she could use to delay going back into the room and slipping beneath the covers on that big, lonely bed.

"It's all yours," she said as she came out. Her voice trailed away when she saw Hal. He'd turned the television so he could see it from his cramped bed on the loveseat. Fully dressed, but without his glasses, he lay curled up, eyes closed. He was asleep.

Lili shivered. The room was now even colder than it had been before the disaster with the radiator. The bed had a wonderfully thick down comforter and deliciously warm flannel sheets. She'd be fine. *But Hal?* Watching him, his face slack with sleep, Lili knew she couldn't leave him there to freeze all night.

"Wake up," she said gently, kneeling next to him.

Hal muttered and his eyelids fluttered, but he didn't wake. She tried again, running her fingers lightly across his forehead. "Wake up, Hal."

With a quick, soft intake of breath, Hal opened his eyes. She knew without his glasses he couldn't see more than a few inches in front of him, so she moved closer. His green eyes focused on her face and he smiled.

"Lili," he said, and she thought he must still be half asleep. He touched her cheek. "My Lili."

Her stomach turned over at his words. "Hal. Wake up!"

He blinked rapidly, then slid his tongue across his lips. It was a gesture so uncontrived, so natural, but at the same time incredibly sensual. Her stomach twisted again.

"Lili?" He sat up, stretching. "I must've dropped off."

"You were asleep," she said unnecessarily.

Hal scratched his head so the hair stood on end. "What time is it?"

The bedside clock said only ten pm. "It's pretty early."

He yawned jaw crackingly. "Man, I'm bushed." Then he shivered. "It's cold in here."

"You go get ready for bed," Lili said. She was glad of something practical to do, something to take her mind of her sudden confusing feelings. "I'll call the front desk and see if they can send someone to fix the radiator before tomorrow morning."

Hal went into the bathroom, and the front desk told her there wouldn't be anyone available until the morning. There was probably an extra blanket in the armoire, the apologetic desk clerk told her. Lili didn't want to say they were already using it for the love seat.

It didn't seem there'd be much choice. She wasn't going to let Hal freeze out here all night long, not when the bed was more than large enough for the two of them. *Sharing the bed makes sense,* Lili told herself. *For warmth.*

When he emerged from the bathroom, Lili pointed to the bed. "I moved your stuff here."

He didn't get it at first, she could tell by the look of confusion. "But…"

She made it easier for both of them. "It's freezing in here, Hal. We can share the bed until they fix the radiator tomorrow. It'll be warmer."

It certainly would, she thought, watching Hal's chest. Despite the chilly room, he'd forgotten his shirt again. She'd never thought much about male nipples before, but now, seeing them tight with cold, Lily kept imagining how they'd taste.

He'd said something to her and she'd missed it. "Sorry?"

"I said, how do you want to do it?"

Was he asking her—what on earth was he asking her? "What?"

Hal pointed. "Do you want to sleep on the side next to the window or the bathroom?"

"Oh." She was too embarrassed to admit her mind had been in the gutter. "Bathroom side, I guess."

They got into bed gingerly. Lili turned out the lights, settled back against her pillow, and tugged the heavy layers of blankets up around her chin. Hal's weight beside her was an unusual sensation, but not uncomfortable. Despite her heightened awareness, the stress of the past few days weighed her eyelids down. She felt herself drifting off to sleep.

Someone dumped a bucket of ice onto her bare calves. Lili yelped and sat up. "What the hell?"

Hal rolled away from her. "My feet. Sorry."

"They're like ice!" Lili grumbled, all vestiges of sleep chased away. "Don't you wear socks to bed?"

"Can't," Hal said matter-of-factly. "It gives me athlete's foot."

Ew. Okay, if the icy feet hadn't banished romantic dreams from her mind, that little revelation sure had. Lili sighed, sinking back into her pillow.

"Just keep them on your own side," she said.

Hal rustled around, shifting the covers and rolling in the bed. Lili waited for him to finish before adjusting her own pillow and share of the blankets. By the time they were done, she was just beginning to feel her eyes slipping shut again.

"Hal!" She shrieked. "Your feet!"

"Sorry," Hal said. "But you're so warm."

"Your own side," Lili warned.

Hal stayed still for a moment before she heard the sound of snapping fingers. "I've got it."

He got out of bed and fumbled around the foot of the bed. She heard him stub his toe, mutter a curse, then finally trip over his suitcase. She heard the zipper, then shuffling. Her heart began pounding again. What was he doing?

Then he was back in bed. She heard the sound of foil crinkling. Lili's heart was going to beat right out of her chest!

"This should help," Hal said.

More foil crinkling.

Lili braced herself. Was he going to kiss her? Or just roll over on top of her and—

"Here," Hal said, slipping something into her hand.

It was hot, whatever it was, and Lili reflexively jerked away. "What is it?"

"It's a hand warmer," Hal said in the darkness. "Why? What did you think it would be?"

A hand warmer. Who on earth packed hand warmers in their suitcase? Hal, that's who. Mr. Eagle Scout. Mr. Prepared.

"Nothing," Lili said and tucked the warm plastic packet down to the foot of the bed. "Good night, Hal."

CHAPTER 7

Lying next to Lili all night should have kept Hal awake, but there had been too many early mornings and uneasy nights lately. He slept like the dead. When he finally awoke, the morning sun shone through the lace curtains and cast a golden glow over the entire room.

His nose felt like an ice cube, but since that was the only thing sticking out from the mountain of covers, everything else was toasty warm. He yawned, stretching, and realized he actually felt—good. His hand didn't encounter a lump under the covers with him. Lili must already be up.

"Good morning," he said to the room. Hal found his glasses on the nightstand and slipped them on, bringing everything into focus.

Lili, wearing a thick, bulky sweater, heavy pants and a scowl, sat on the loveseat. She had her hands wrapped around a mug of some dark beverage, and it steamed in the room's frosty air. She didn't look happy.

"Good morning?" The greeting had become a question. Despite his current career, Hal didn't know much about women, in general, but he did know how to recognize one in a state of irritation.

Lili humphed and sipped at the drink. She winced, touching her lip. "Hot!"

"Have you been up long?"

It was the wrong question. "I don't know," Lili said with false sweetness. "Do you consider all night to be long?"

"You didn't sleep well," Hal said, not asked.

74

"You could say that," Lili replied.

He knew it had to be his fault. "What'd I do?" he asked resignedly.

"You snored," she said. "You muttered. You rolled around a lot. You hogged the covers."

"I get the picture," Hal said.

Lili set her mug down on the dresser. "I'm going for breakfast. Are you coming?"

"Just let me get dressed," Hal said, already out of bed and pulling on his jeans.

Lili let out a sigh so longsuffering Hal knew her long list of complaints was not the only reason she was mad this morning. But darned if he could figure out why. He'd stayed on his own side of the bed, for the most part any way. He hadn't made any wrong moves and hadn't tried to touch her.

"Lili," he said finally as he buttoned his shirt. "What's wrong? Why are you really mad at me today?"

"Mad?" She said, shoving her arm into her coat sleeve so hard some threads popped. "What on earth gives you the idea I'm mad at you?"

He pulled on a sweatshirt, then some socks. Matching. "You seem mad."

"I'm just tired," she said shortly. "I didn't sleep well last night."

"Because of me," he said.

"Yes," Lili replied, glaring.

"Because I snored," Hal offered, still trying to figure out her real reason.

"Because—because you slept!" Lili fumed.

Fortunately, the bed was close enough for him to sit on. Hal sat, completely perplexed. "What?"

She threw her hands in the air. "Forget it!"

Even as she headed toward the door, Hal reached out and caught her by the wrist. She didn't struggle too hard to get away. She even let him turn her so she faced him.

"What's going on?" he asked.

"You slept all night long," Lili said, as though she were admitting some terrible secret.

He frowned, not—quite—getting it. "And?"

She sighed in frustration. "I thought you might...I wanted you to...oh, just forget it!"

Her cheeks were pink like she was embarrassed. Hal still didn't understand. "You didn't want me to sleep?"

"No!" She shouted. Then, softer, "No."

"What did you want— Oh." Hal could have kicked himself for being so blind. Now it was his turn to be embarrassed. He dropped Lili's wrist and pushed off from the bed. All at once he felt like he needed to pace.

"Let's just go, okay?" Lili almost pleaded. She headed toward the door again, her back straight like she had a poker stuck down her pants.

"If I had known," Hal began.

"Well, obviously you didn't," Lili said formally, pausing before she opened the door. "I'm sorry I brought it up. Forget it."

But he couldn't forget it, not when images of how the night could have been spent kept pushing their way into his head. If he hadn't been so blind. If he hadn't been stupid!

"Let's go," Lili said and opened the door. Hal followed her out because there wasn't much else he could do.

*   *   *

Breakfast was sawdust in Lili's mouth. It was hard to eat through a forced smile, especially when she felt like crying. *What had I expected anyway?* she berated herself. Muriel Whitehead had told her up front that no Lovematch escort ever initiated sexual intimacy with a client, unless it was clearly and obviously stated to be the client's desire.

And I had desired it, she thought as she followed the crowd out of the morning dining room. Hal's kiss after the carriage ride had awakened a passion in her she'd thought dead after losing Ian. She'd had few dates in the three years since Ian's death, and none of those men had made her feel the way Hal did.

"Walleyball?" Eli asked, catching up to her. "Bubbe and Zayde rented the court until lunchtime. Ready to play?"

The last thing Lili wanted to do was to join one of the infamous Alster sports tournaments. But she was here to enjoy family fun time, and it would prevent her from having to spend time alone with Hal. She managed a weak smile of agreement.

"Sure."

Eli looked at her closely. "Lili, are you okay?"

Lili looked over her shoulder. Hal was walking alone, and she knew she should go back and keep him company. "Don't start, Eli. Please."

"If he's done anything to you—"

She took her brother's hand for a minute. "I'm fine. I told Ruth the same thing. Please, believe me."

"We just want to see you happy," her brother muttered.

His emotional admittance touched her. "I know."

"We all liked Ian," Elijah said gruffly. "He was a good guy."

"Hal's a good guy, too," Lili said.

Elijah looked confused. "Who?"

"David," Lili said quickly. "I said he's a good guy, too."

"It sounded like—"

"Hey, I'll meet you at the court!" Lili countered and waved him off. She fell back until Hal caught up with her. "You up for walleyball?"

"Never played." Hal took her hand and they both waved at all the family members who were now staring at them suspiciously.

"It's like volleyball but in a racquetball court," Lili explained. She tried to ignore the way Hal's grasp on her palm made her heart race, but couldn't.

"I'm pretty bad at volleyball."

Ian would never have admitted to being bad at anything, Lili thought suddenly. And if he had, wouldn't she have thought less of him? But coming from Hal, the admission didn't sound so bad, so unmanly. It just sounded honest.

"Join the club," Lili said. "Maybe we should be on different teams."

Hal stopped, and since he still held her hand, Lili stopped, too.

"Are you sure you want me to play?"

His question was so serious she couldn't give him a joking answer. "Of course I do."

"I just thought..." He shrugged. "You might not want me around."

"Hurry up, you two!" That was Bubbe calling from the entrance to the sports building. "Shake your bon-bons!"

"Listen," Lili said, then sighed. She wasn't quite sure what she wanted to say. "Forget about what I said this morning. I wasn't thinking right. I was just tired. We only have two more days to get through, and then you can leave."

"Yeah, right," Hal said without enthusiasm.

"So let's go in there and play walleyball," Lili said, equally unenthusiastic. "And Hal?"

"Hmmm?" He asked, already starting to walk again.

"You have to start being mean. Meaner."

He stopped again. "Meaner?"

Lili nodded firmly. "Be a real jerk. They've got to really hate you by the time we break up. I don't want anyone telling me I need to give you another chance."

"They already hate me," Hal muttered with a look at the sports building. "They think I beat you, for Heaven's sakes!"

She could tell he was uncomfortable playing the bad guy, and no wonder. Hal was just about the most decent man she'd ever met. Unfortunately, she didn't need a nice, decent guy. She needed a real jerk.

"It's time to get tough," she said. "Can you make them hate you without having them make death threats?"

Her attempt at humor fell flat. "I'll try," Hal said grimly.

"They're waiting," Lili said. "Let's go."

It was like they were going into battle. Hal's grip grew firm, then almost painful, until he finally dropped her hand at the door to the building. Didn't just drop it, in fact, but threw it away from him. He took a deep breath and squared his shoulders.

Lili opened the door, assaulted instantly by the shouts and sounds of shoes squeaking on the wooden floors. Two racquetball courts ran along side the large, open gymnasium set up with basketball hoops, ping pong tables and other play equipment. She found the court marked Alster and pointed.

"In there."

Hal gave her a look so contemptuous it actually made her take a step back. "I can read."

"Oh." Lili's voice was small. "Sorry."

Instantly, Hal's cold sneer turned to a concerned frown. "I was just practicing," he whispered.

"Oh," Lili repeated. *Of course.*

They opened the door and faced the enemy. *Er, my family,* Lili corrected herself. She saw two empty spots in the lineup on the other side of the net, and she directed Hal toward them.

"I hope you're better at this than you were last time," he remarked loudly as they ducked beneath the net and took their spots.

The game started without preamble. Her brother, Michael, served for the other team. "Zero serving zero!"

The ball rocketed over the net, coming down directly over Lili's head. She put her hands up to hit it, but misjudged the distance and it undershot her. She watched it bounce mere inches from her feet, earning the other team its first point.

"That's my Lili," Hal said, loud enough for everyone to hear. "Way to go, Lil."

She ignored him, shaking off the urge to defend herself. Hal was just playing a character. *He didn't,* she reassured herself, *really mean anything by it.*

"One serving zero!"

The game began in earnest with both sides playing hard. The spirit in the room was competitive, but fun. Lili's younger cousins ribbed each other good-naturedly when anyone goofed up, and since the skill levels of those playing went from athletic genius to fumbling klutz, there was a lot of ribbing. Bubbe and Zayde watched from the glass-protected loft above the room, calling out encouragement and video taping the entire thing.

"Nice one, Lil," Hal said sarcastically when Lili's attempt at spiking the ball sent it flying into the net. "Real nice."

Though the same words had come out of her cousin Charlie's mouth just moments before, from Hal, the comment bit and stung. Again Lili shrugged it off, knowing he was only doing as she'd asked. The ball flew toward her again, but Hal stepped in front of her to slam it back across the net. *And he'd said he wasn't any good at the game?*

"I was going to get that," Lili blurted.

"Sure you were, sweetheart," Hal said and rolled his eyes. "Just like you got the last one. Here's a clue, baby. The ball's suppose to go *over* the net."

Lili bit her tongue to stop a sharp retort. She wasn't a bad player. In fact, once she got warmed up, she bordered on being pretty darn good.

He's only doing what I told him, she reminded herself. She searched Hal's eyes for a flicker of warmth, of the man who'd kissed her under the stars. All she saw was patronizing contempt.

The game got more intense with people flying all over the court trying to outdo one another. The ball sprang off walls and ricocheted around the room as the players got better at the game. Lili, despite Hal's repeated jibes, really began to enjoy herself.

However, the better she got, the worse Hal's comments became. When she finally managed to spike a ball, she turned to high-five Charlie and her other teammates. Hal merely said, "It's about time."

He called her Butterfingers when she fumbled a serve. He told everyone to make sure they covered their eyes so they wouldn't go blind when she bent over to retrieve a ball that had gone out of bounds. Worst of all, he laughed when she slipped and fell during one particularly valiant attempt at returning a serve.

With every comment, Lili grew angrier. Now he was just being downright nasty. Though they didn't say much, she could tell her family members weren't appreciating Hal's acid remarks either. Eli in particular kept scowling at him. Lili hoped her brother wasn't going to take it upon herself to be her defender.

The second game, if possible, was worse than the first. Though everyone else laughed and joked, Hal kept berating her. If she missed a shot, he mocked her. If she made a shot, he told her how she could have done it better.

"Why not just stand there and let me do all the work?" he asked her after she'd stepped back to let him take a shot she knew she wasn't going to reach. "Oh, wait. That's just what you're doing already."

Hot tears burned her eyes and she fought them back. She'd told him to be mean, and he was giving her what she'd asked for. She rolled her shoulders and her neck, trying to relieve the tension. Her earlier enjoyment was rapidly fading. She was glad the game was almost over.

"Fourteen to thirteen!" Eli called, setting up the serve.

The ball sailed over the net like it had wings. It came straight toward her, and Lili put up her hands. She was in perfect form, ready to slam that ball over the net and earn her team the next serve.

She never had the chance. Hal barreled into her, his own hands in the air. His feet trod on her toes, filling her with a pain so intense it was almost sublime. His weight knocked her to the floor on her hands and knees.

"Yes!" Hal yelled, pumping his fist in the air. He'd slammed the ball down on the other side of the net and nobody had gone after it.

Everyone rushed to Lili's side, helping her to her feet. *If I ever forget why I love my family,* Lili thought a little blearily, *I'll remember this day.*

One of her cousins pressed a paper cup of water into her hand. Another helped her limp over the bench along the wall. Still others gathered around to ask her questions about how she felt.

"You shouldn't be playing such a rough game in your condition," clucked her normally quiet sister-in-law, Sarah.

Lili would have asked her what she meant, but she didn't have a chance with the rest of her cousins clamoring to help her lift her feet, lower her head, or vice versa.

She wasn't bleeding anywhere and even the pain in her toes had begun to fade. Lili finally waved away all the helping hands, saying she was fine. She was fine. The game was over, though, the fun mood spoiled, and she did regret she'd been the cause of that.

"I'm fine, really!" she said for what felt like the hundredth time. At last she convinced the crowd to disperse, which they did reluctantly.

"*Bubbeleh,* come with us to the movie lounge," Bubbe urged. "We're going to watch that little cutie Keanu Reeves in that football movie."

Lili didn't have the heart to tell her bubbe that the actor's name was not pronounced canoe. Besides, she really didn't want to watch a movie right now. She really just wanted to go back to her room, take a long, hot bath, and curl up in bed. As gracefully as she could, she declined Bubbe's offer, then looked around for Hal.

He was gone.

*　　　*　　　*

The fallen leaves crunched crisply under Hal's feet as he trudged along the path. He had no scarf or gloves, but he had his humiliation to keep him warm. He passed the fork in the path that would take him back to Bramblewood's main building and kept going. He needed to think.

Since Cassie ran off with his ex-partner John, Hal's only brush with real romance had been with the client who'd bought him the book of love poems. Other than that, the dates he'd had were work, not pleasure. Until meeting Lili, none of the LoveMatch women had been anything more than a way to pay the bills.

She's just a client, he told himself fiercely. *This is just a job.* She wanted him to be a jerk, so he had been. But he hadn't meant to knock her down, not during the game or any of the times his clumsiness had gotten the best of him.

And why had she been so upset when he hadn't tried to seduce her? It was strict LoveMatch policy that no escort was to make a sexual advance unless the client clearly stated that was what she wanted. No escort was required to provide sexual services, either, unless he wanted to.

He thought guiltily of the kiss he'd given her after the carriage ride. It was certainly a mistake. He'd allowed himself to forget he was working. He'd let himself believe what he was pretending to have with Lili was the real thing. *But it wasn't the real thing,* Hal thought, with a kick to a pile of leaves that connected with a hidden tree root and started him hopping in pain.

Hal limped down the path. If he'd met Lili someplace else, some other way? But who was he kidding? He had nothing to offer any woman, much less one like Lili. He had no real job, no car; and he lived in a one-bedroom apartment with shabby furniture and not much more than mold and water in the refrigerator.

Once he'd owned his own business, had a nice house, and driven an expensive car. Losing Cassie, he lost all that, too. Alone, it hadn't mattered. He'd gone back to school to finally do something he thought he'd enjoy.

But now—now he looked at the bleak existence he'd been eking out for the past year, and wondered how he even dared imagine that he could start a relationship with someone he truly cared about. He could barely afford to take her to a fast food burger joint, much less a nice restaurant.

Hal finally turned back toward Bramblewood's main grounds. Night was falling fast, and he was getting cold. He'd go back and face Lili, apologize once again for being such an incredible klutz, and hope she'd forgive him. Yet again.

Fortunately, he didn't pass any of the Alster clan on the way back to the room. He didn't think he could face any of them right now. Since Lili had the only room key, he hoped she was in. He knocked.

After a few minutes, she answered. To his relief, there were no fresh bruises he could see. She must have been in the bath because she wore the room's thick, complimentary robe and had bundled her hair into a towel.

"Where have you been?" she asked, letting him in. "I've been worried."

"I went for a walk," Hal told her. He slipped off his coat and hung it up. He looked around the room, wincing. It was a mess. Half the contents of his suitcase lay scattered all over the floor. He started picking things up and shoving them back in the overburdened case.

"It's getting dark," Lili said quietly. "I was afraid you'd gotten lost or something."

"Yeah, that would be just like me, wouldn't it?" Hal said bitterly, shoving a pair of jeans into the suitcase. "Big idiot that I am."

"That's not what I meant."

He paused, shoulders drooping. "You really hired the wrong man for this job, Lili."

"You think so?" She sat down on the bed to watch him stuff the suitcase. "I don't. I needed someone to make my family happy I was still single. I'd say you did a great job of that today."

He risked a glance at her. "You're not mad?"

She bit her lip, a gesture he found unbelieveably appealing. "I was. You said some pretty rude things. Again."

Hal sighed and went back to the task of tidying the room. "I'm only trying to do what you asked me to."

"I know that." Lili smiled. "And I am grateful."

"Even though I've nearly killed you a bunch of times already?"

Now she laughed out loud. "I could've done without that. I'm still sore."

"I could give you a massage." The offer slipped out without him thinking about it. Once the words were out, though, all that filled his mind were thoughts of Lili, naked and covered in oil under his hands.

"Could you?" She rolled her neck, wincing. "That would really be great!"

"I need the practice," Hal admitted. "Especially since I'm missing some classes this week."

"Where do you want me?" Lili asked. She patted the bed. "Here?"

Oh, that sure would be a good place to start. Hal gave himself a mental shake. "Sure."

She paused. "Clothes on? Or off?"

"Most people prefer to wear a towel," Hal said, forcing his voice not to betray the way her question had sent his heart pounding.

Lili pulled the one from her head, letting her hair down. "Okay."

"Wait just a minute." Hal rifled through the suitcase until he found what he wanted. "My oil."

"You really do have everything in there," she marveled.

"I'll go into the bathroom," Hal offered. "Just let me know when you're ready."

He was only in the room a minute when she called for him to return. She'd turned out all the lights but one, and turned the radio to a station playing light classical music. She'd pulled the covers back and now lay face down on the robe, covered by a towel from her waist to her knees.

Hal put an extra towel next to her head. "I brought this for you."

"See, that's what I like about you, Hal," Lili said almost sleepily. "You think of everything."

He started by drizzling some oil onto her bare back. Lili gasped at the chill of it; it had been in his suitcase and not a warmer. Not the way his instructors would like, but the best he could do under the circumstances.

It warmed quickly beneath his fingers. Hal rubbed Lili's back in long, firm strokes, concentrating on running his thumbs just beside the ridge of her spine. She let out a little groan/moan, a sound so filled with pure pleasure it made Hal's mouth go dry.

"That is excellent," Lili said. "Wow. Wow!"

"This is why I want to be a massage therapist," Hal said. "I want to make people feel good."

"It's working," she mumbled.

He kept up the massage, using all the techniques they'd gone over in class. Somehow, performing the massage on his classmates was incredibly different from working on Lili. For one thing, she was a lot more vocal with her appreciation.

"Oh, yes," she moaned.

Hal's mind wanted to imagine her saying those words in that tone while his hands performed a different sort of massage. He forced the thoughts away. If he wanted to be a professional, he couldn't let his attraction to the client affect his performance!

It was hard to ignore Lili's low moans of pleasure, though, or to not imagine them as coming from a different source. She practically started purring when he began working her shoulders and neck, easing the tension out of them with strong, smooth strokes. *Concentrate on the hands,* Hal thought. *Concentrate.*

"You've got magic hands." Lili's voice had gone low and throaty. "God, Hal, you're good!"

She wriggled a little under his touch. Her back had taken on a sheer, rosy glow from all his ministrations. He thought, *That's how her skin would look flushed with passion, too.*

He had to stop or he'd embarrass himself. "I think that's it," he said.

"No," she wailed in complaint, sitting up.

She clutched the towel Hal had given her to her chest, but he still knew she was naked. He backed off the bed hastily, turning around. He made a great pretense of putting away the oil and wiping his hands before daring to turn around.

She hadn't put her robe back on. Her dark hair caressed her shoulders. Lili's eyes were glazed, her lips as plump and pink as if she'd just been kissed.

Baseball, Hal thought furiously. *Hockey. World Series. Stanley Cup. Games on the big screen TV at Hooters—hooters—no! Cold showers. Aunt Millie in her bathing suit—*

"Hal," Lili said. "Come here."

His mind screamed no, but his feet said yes. They led him to where Lili sat. She patted the bed, and he sat where she wanted him.

"I know the LoveMatch rules," she said in a husky voice. "Ms. Whitehead was very clear about what an escort will and will not do."

Hal coughed. "Uh-huh."

Lili smiled enigmatically. He could see the euphoria of the massage still lingering in the glaze of her eyes and the way she licked her lips. She looked a little drunk. *I did that,* Hal thought, and his body responded.

"Hal?"

"Yes, Lili."

"Why did you kiss me after the carriage ride?"

He found it hard to speak with a mouth that wanted nothing else but to kiss her again. "Because I wanted to."

"Do you want to now?" Lili asked.

He nodded, unable to answer.

"Then do it," Lili breathed. "Please."

If he'd had any other ideas, they fled from his mind as if they were shadows facing the noonday sun. Kissing Lili was better than eating ice cream on a summer day. Slipping between flannel sheets on a cold night. Having his hair washed by a beautician with strong fingers. Every pleasure in Hal's life paled in comparison to the feeling of Lili's lips on his.

"Are you sure?" He found the strength to ask, needing to hear the confirmation.

She didn't say anything. Instead, she dropped her towel. Hal took that as a yes.

CHAPTER 8

When Hal kissed Lili, he did it as though they were the only two people in the entire world. He made it easy for her to block everything out, to lose herself in the sensations sweeping over her. That was what Lili wanted to do. Lose herself.

He paused only briefly to take his glasses off and put them on the nightstand. Lili took the opportunity to catch her breath. That was when she noticed she was completely naked and he was still fully clothed.

"This won't work," she said.

Hal sighed. His shoulders slumped. "I knew you were going to say that."

He did? Lili shook her head and reached out to tug on the front of his shirt. "No, Hal. I mean that this won't work with you still dressed."

She figured she must be nothing more than a vague blur to him, so she moved closer. His mouth was sweet, his lips full and soft. She loved the feeling of his smoothly shaved face against her own.

Alone in the steaming hot bathtub, waiting for Hal to return, she'd thought about doing this. Since Ian's death, Lili's life had been devoid of passion, of intimacy. Making love to Hal would finally set her free from the cage of guilt she'd trapped herself in three years before.

His mouth left hers to trail along her jaw, then down to the exquisitely tender spot just below her ear. Lili shivered, clutching at his shoulders. He knew just where to kiss her, how to touch her, just as if he'd taken classes. *And who knows?* she thought a little foolishly. *Maybe he had.*

"Lili," Hal whispered in her ear. "I need to know you're sure about this."

"I'm sure."

She'd never been more certain about anything in her life. She couldn't go on living in the past, grieving for a love that hadn't blossomed. The guilt she felt over Ian's death had far too long kept her from seeking and finding joy. What she and Hal might have tonight wouldn't— couldn't—be permanent. It wasn't love. But it would be close enough.

Now his mouth trailed along the curve of her collarbone, and when he flicked his tongue along her skin, Lili could not stifle a cry. He pulled away, working at the buttons on his shirt with fumbling fingers. A button popped off, hitting her spang in the chest.

"Let me," Lili said. "Let's get through this without injury, okay?"

He did laugh, and that was one of the reasons Lili knew her decision to open herself to him had been right. Hal was a good man. A kind man. She could let him love her, just for tonight, and know that even though it wasn't the real thing, he would be able to make her believe it was. It was the LoveMatch guarantee.

She pushed his shirt off his shoulders and ran her fingers along the broad plane of his chest. His muscles jumped and twitched under her touch as she circled his taut male nipples with her fingertips. Driven by an urge she didn't understand and didn't want to think about, Lili dipped her head to put her tongue on the places her fingers had just caressed.

Hal's groan was inspiration enough for her to continue. He caught his fingers in her hair as she lavished kisses along his chest and down further, following the line of crisp, crinkly hair to where it disappeared into the waistband of his jeans. Lili paused there, for just one moment, thinking that if she wanted to turn back, now would be the time.

She didn't want to turn back. She found the button and unhooked it, slid the zipper down and opened his jeans. Hal wore purple briefs, a sight so surprising Lili sat back.

"Purple?" She asked.

He looked down. "I like purple."

"I like purple, too," Lili said. "But I'd prefer to see them on the floor."

Her bold words shocked herself into a chuckle. Being with Hal made her feel bubbly, giddy. Lighthearted, she realized. Like she was having fun.

She helped him push off his cumbersome jeans and socks, but stopped before helping him remove his last piece of clothing. Lili had never been shy about lovemaking. She was confident with her body and how it reacted, and she was assured enough to know she could please a man. But something about this last step made her pause.

Hal didn't give her time to think. He pulled her close for another kiss, wrapping his arms around her. He caressed her back, still slick with oil. Every slide of his fingers against her skin electrified her.

She opened her mouth and their tongues met. Hal didn't stab her with his tongue. He didn't force her mouth wide. His every movement was gentle and exactly what she needed and wanted, just when she wanted it.

Slowly, Hal pushed her back onto the mound of pillows, but he didn't lay on top of her. They lay on their sides, facing each other, and he slid his leg between hers. The feeling of his thigh against her naked sex made her gasp. She was on fire.

She ran her hands along his smooth, strong back, letting her fingers learn every sensitive part of him. All the while, their mouths danced together in kisses so exactly perfect she had to wonder if she was just dreaming all of this.

When her hands encountered the waistband of his briefs, she knew this was real. No dream would come with persistent purple underpants. Lili hooked her fingers inside the waistband, easing them over his lean hips and down his sturdy thighs. They never stopped kissing, not even when she used her foot to finally push the bulky briefs all the way off.

Lili was glad she'd left the lamp on. Seeing Hal naked was worth it. His body was lovely, perfectly formed and golden brown in the dim lamplight. The hair around his rising erection was darker than on his head, a springy tuft that crinkled softly against her belly.

He groaned softly as she pulled their bodies apart to look at him. "Lili—"

"Shhh," she said. "I want to see you."

He shivered in response, and he bent his head to the hollow of her shoulder. Now it was her turn to gasp as his tongue found her skin. They rolled together again, Hal's leg slipping further between hers. He ran his hand down her back to cup her buttocks, pressing her more firmly onto his thigh.

The pressure was delightful, incredible. Erotic. Lili rocked against him and was rewarded when his mouth slanted across hers again. Hal's kisses became more urgent, more focused as she let her own hand slide down to caress the firm bulge of his rear end.

Lili hooked her leg over his calf, locking them together. Hal's erection rose hotly against her stomach. Suddenly she wanted to touch it. Lili pushed their bodies apart again so she could slip her fingers around his arousal.

"Oh, Hal," she whispered when he jerked beneath her touch. "You're so lovely."

Ian would have scolded her for using such a feminine adjective to describe the part he held in highest esteem. Hal didn't say anything. His only answer a short moan. It pleased Lili to think she'd caused him to become incapable of speech.

She ran her fingers lightly up and down along his length. With a sigh, Hal rolled onto his back and crossed his arms up high, over his eyes. He was even more magnificent in full view. Lili marveled that a man who seemed so unassuming, so unpretentious, could be built so perfectly and not boast about it.

She knew he was tall, but seeing him stretched out on the bed made his legs seem impossibly long. His flat stomach tapered to lean hips, with bones that jutted just enough to make her want to lick them. Lili did just that, bending to run her tongue along the curved surface of bone. His hair tickled her nose.

It gave her pleasure to watch the way his mouth tightened when she brushed her fingers along the inside of his thigh. His penis stiffened further as she watched. She encircled him with her fingers, soaking in the sight and smells of his body.

"Enough," Hal said hoarsely. He sat up, taking her hand gently away from where it had been playing. "I need to slow down."

Lili nodded, feeling the same way. She throbbed with a need so intense it was almost frightening. *And all from touching him.* What was she going to do when he began to touch her?

She soon found out. Hal pushed her back onto the pillows again. He kissed her once, lightly, on the mouth, then moved lower. He didn't stop at her throat this time, but pressed his mouth to the first curves of her breasts, one at a time. Lili felt her nipples peak under the torturous gentleness of his breath against them. Then the hot weight of his tongue, swirling first around one, then the other. He suckled gently, bringing forth a startled gasp from her.

"Do you want me to stop?" he asked, concerned.

"Good Lord, no!" Lili cried.

Hal dropped more kisses onto her breasts, then moved down along the soft curve of her belly. He kissed her thighs, her knees, down her calves to the tops of her feet, her ankles. Even her toes got his full attention, as he kissed them until she laughed out loud at the tickling that also sent shock waves of pleasure directly to her swollen center.

He moved again to her thighs, parting them with gentle pressure. Lili waited, breathless, uncertain if she should move. Uncertain if she could stop herself from moving. She felt his hot breath against her. He dropped a kiss onto the nest of her hair. He stopped. She waited. He kissed her again as though waiting to judge her reaction.

Lili sighed, opening herself to him. He kissed her, darting his tongue out like a butterfly tasting a flower. Lili gave herself up to the sensations rocketing through her. *It has been so long, so long!*

It seemed like hours but was only minutes that Hal made love to her with his mouth. Lili tossed on a sea of feeling that rose and fell. When he pulled away from her, she felt helpless to speak in protest, such was her daze. The bed was cold without him on it, and she heard the crinkling of foil again. *No handwarmers this time,* she had time to think before Hal returned.

He slid up the length of her, pressing his body to hers. His heat slipped inside her, stretching her to delicious tautness. He moved, slowly, and she urged him on by clutching her hands to his buttocks. Her mouth found his chest as he rocked inside her and she tongued his nipples again, relishing the way he shuddered at her every touch.

"Lili," he whispered in a voice so thick with passion she scarcely recognized it.

Yet still she couldn't answer him, even though his name was throbbing on the tip of her tongue, begging to be set free. She moaned instead, tilting her head to allow his kisses access to her throat. Lili moved her hips in time with Hal's thrusts, letting him set the pace, but meeting him equally.

She let her hands explore the firm muscles of his forearms, then up to his shoulders and down his sides. Sweat covered him, oiling her fingers and making their bodies slippery against each other.

She was close, so close. Her thighs fluttered as every thrust sent her closer and closer to the edge she'd denied herself for so long. Her orgasm hit her like glass shattering, sending shards of exquisite sensation rippling through her entire body and at last forcing a word from her lips.

"Hal!" Lili cried then sank her teeth into his shoulder.

Hal hissed in pain and she backed off, the sharp and clear blasts of pleasure still rocketing through her. He murmured her name over and over, and this time she answered him. He mumbled words of love and she replied, knowing in some small part of her mind that neither of them could possible mean what they said. Not now, not with sex shooting through their veins like bullets from a gun.

Hal let out one last, hoarse moan and his entire body rippled. He sank down onto her, and Lili expected him to be heavy. Instead, just like everything else about tonight, she discovered he was a perfect fit.

*   *   *

Hal awoke to the sound of Lili singing in the bathroom. He heard water running the tub. It turned off. More singing, slightly off tune and a completely wacky choice of song, and then some splashing.

If he hadn't had the voice of a male elk during mating season, Hal would have chosen *Oh, What A Beautiful Morning,* from the show *Oklahoma,* to describe his mood. Oddly enough, Lili was singing *The Time Warp.*

Maybe that jump to the left was what made all that splashing, Hal thought, and decided to check it out. He didn't bother knocking. Two people who got naked and sweaty together didn't have much to hide from each other.

"'Morning," he said, heading straight for the toilet. He commenced to relieve himself of the world's fullest bladder, sighing in relief. "Whew. I thought I was going to float away."

Lili wasn't singing anymore. Hal finished his business, making sure to put the seat back down, and turned toward the tub. She'd sunk into the water and covered her eyes.

"Lili?" he asked, concerned.

"You—you're—" She spluttered. "Couldn't you wait to do that?"

"Truthfully? No," Hal said, washing his hands at the sink. "I was about to burst."

"Are you done?" she demanded, peeking through her fingers.

"Sure." Hal stuck his fingers in the water and splashed her playfully. "Room in here for one more?"

"No!" Lili kicked her foot out at him. "And I'd appreciate it if you'd give me some privacy!"

Hal gave himself a mental kick. Apparently he'd overstepped the bounds of male/female morning-after etiquette. He left the bathroom without even brushing his teeth.

Her reaction surprised him. Last night, Lili had been all over him, initiating sex in the way required by LoveMatch rules. But Hal hadn't made love to Lili out of a sense of duty. He'd wanted to taste her, feel her, bring her pleasure.

He slipped into a pair of old sweatpants and a T-shirt, wishing he'd had a chance in the bath. Lili appeared in the doorway, entirely covered by the robe and a towel wrapped around her hair. It might have been a pleasant reminder of the way she'd been dressed last night, except for her distant look and thinned lips.

"It's all yours," she said, indicating the bathroom, but Hal didn't go in.

He had to try one more thing, something that would be a sign Lili had come to him out of her desire for him...Hal. Not just as the man she'd hired to scratch an itch.

He reached out and snagged her arm as she tried to squeeze by him, then pulled her into his arms. Kissing her was like kissing a stick of wood. She stood stiffly in his embrace, not fighting or pulling away, but not responding.

Hal had his answer. "All right," he said with as much dignity as he could. "I'll be out in a few minutes."

He didn't have to run the cold water in the tub this morning. Lili's cool demeanor and lack of response had cooled him down more than enough. He scrubbed his skin harshly, wishing he could wash away the memory of her hands on him. It didn't work.

He brushed his teeth so fiercely he spat pink-tinged toothpaste into the bowl. He rinsed and spat again, trying to rinse away the taste of humiliation coating his tongue. That didn't work either.

LoveMatch training included specialized courses in how to respond to a client who requested sexual favors. Escorts could always turn down a client wanting more from them than just a kiss on the doorstep. Most of the guys, like Rick, considered sex a bonus above and beyond the monetary. Hal had always considered himself lucky if his date didn't slap him by the end of the night.

None of the men Hal worked with ever talked about wanting to make love to the women who hired them. For them, it was just a job, another skill they learned like how to order the right wine or tie a French cravat. Consequently, none of the LoveMatch locker room bragging had ever been about what it was like to realize the woman they'd just spent the night falling in love with thought of them as nothing more than hired help.

It was just that he'd thought from what she'd said up front that Lili's motives for employing him were straightforward. Play the ignoramus for her family, then break up with her so they'd leave her alone about starting to date again. It wasn't supposed to include hearing her moan his name in passion.

Hal ran wet hands through his hair until it looked almost as dark as his mood. He didn't like being used. Cassie had used him. John had used him. Because of them, he hadn't let himself get close enough to anyone who might use him again. *Until Lili.*

No more. Hal shook his head, spraying water everywhere. Lili hired him to treat her badly. He had a job to do, and he would do it. With enthusiasm.

*   *   *

Lili waited for Hal to take her hand as they headed for breakfast. He didn't. He didn't wait for her either, and his much longer legs kept her scurrying to keep up.

Since coming out of the bathroom this morning, he'd said nothing. If he looked at her, his gaze traveled smoothly across her face and slipped away without meeting her eyes. Lili didn't know how to breach the seemingly impossible distance between them.

Last night had been a mistake of monumental proportions. She saw that now. Foolishly, she'd believed that making love with Hal would finally put the past behind her, help her erase her guilt about Ian. How could she have been so foolish?

It wasn't until seeing him so casually sharing the bathroom with her this morning that she'd balked. Sharing a bed was one thing. Sharing something as intimate and personal as a bathroom seemed quite another. She'd panicked, totally overreacting.

Lili wasn't ready to share herself with a man. Not with the memories of Ian only beginning to fade. He'd taken so much of her that, even after his death, it had taken her three years just to find herself again. She wasn't ready to give that up now.

Hal deserved better than a woman who opened her body to him, but not her heart. He'd told her how badly his ex-wife's betrayal hurt him. How could Lili have ignored that in favor of pursuing her own desires?

"You go ahead," Hal told her. His voice was so different from the one moaning her name last night that Lili wanted to cry. "I've got some things I need to do."

She didn't ask him to explain, and couldn't find her voice to reply. Lili just nodded, then watched him walk away toward the registration desk. Hal walked in the stiff-legged manner of a man who's just been whacked between the legs with a stick. *In a way,* she thought miserably, *that's just what I've done.*

"*Bubbeleh,* you're going to miss breakfast." Bubbe popped out of the ladies' room door, patting her gray bouffant. "And it's French toast today! Your favorite! Remember when I used to make you kids the faces with the French toast and the fruit slices?"

Bubbe's voice trailed off when she noticed Lili wasn't answering. "So, you're going to tell your Bubbe why the long face, or what?"

"It's nothing," Lili lied. She forced a smile. "C'mon. I'm starving."

Bubbe wagged her finger. "It's that nogoodnick David, isn't it? Mr. Big Shot Doctor? What's he done to you this time?"

She had done it to him. "Nothing, Bubbe. Come on."

Bubbe sighed, then put her arm around Lili's shoulders. With a start, Lili realized that the woman who'd loomed so large in her childhood memories had grown impossibly tiny. Bubbe nearly had to stand on tiptoe to reach Lili.

"Lili, you can't hide anything from your Bubbe. You know that. From your mother—*oy!* For her, you can paint the smile and pretend your tears are only dry contact lenses, but Bubbe knows all the tricks."

Despite her misery, Lili had to laugh. "We had a fight. That's all."

Bubbe huffed. "About what?"

"Nothing," Lili said. "You know how it is."

"Your *Zayde* Saul, God love him, he's never argued with me. Not once in sixty years. Can you believe that?"

"No," Lili replied.

Bubbe laughed and pinched her cheek. "Of course we argue. Mostly about nothing. It's when the nothing becomes everything that you have to worry."

Lili sighed, thinking of Ian. "I know."

"We just want you to be happy," *Bubbe* said, squeezing Lili's shoulders again. "It's been a long time since we lost poor Ian, may he rest in peace. It's time you moved on with your life. But we want you to be happy."

"I know you do, *Bubbe,*" Lili said. She gave her grandmother a grateful squeeze.

Bubbe pulled her gently toward a pair of the large overstuffed chairs in front of the fireplace. "Sit, Lili. Talk to your *Bubbe.* It'll make you feel better."

Talking to *Bubbe* always did make her feel better, but this time Lili knew she couldn't open up to her grandmother. Not without spilling the whole awful tower of lies she'd built. Lili's guilt grew in monstrous proportion as she looked into *Bubbe's* concerned eyes. She'd lied to her family, and why? To make them stop bugging her about leaving behind a relationship she had left behind before it ended.

"Lili?" *Bubbe* was waiting for her to answer.

"I don't have much to say, *Bubbe*. We had a fight. That's all. It's nothing I really want to talk about," Lili said.

Bubbe leaned forward to put her hand on Lili's. "Are you sure there isn't something you need to tell me? Your mother's concerned. Eli told her—"

"Eli told her what?" Lili asked suspiciously.

Bubbe sat back in the chair and looked at Lili calmly. It was the same look she'd always given when, as kids, they'd stolen the cookies from the jar. It was an expression designed to force admissions of guilt from even the most reluctant parties.

Lili didn't waver. "There's nothing, *Bubbe!*"

Bubbe sighed, looking sad. "You know you can come to me for anything, *bubbeleh*. Any reason. We're your family, doll. We love you. No matter what."

Did they suspect Lili was lying about Hal? Her heart thumped a little harder and her palms felt sweaty. She wiped them on her pants legs, knowing eagle-eyed *Bubbe* would spot the motion and her nervousness.

"And if it's money you need, *Zayde* Saul and I have already talked about it. We were planning on giving all you kids equal portions in our wills, but if you need it now, we can arrange that."

Money? Lili frowned. "Why on earth would I need money? Ian left me plenty." There wouldn't be much left after paying the LoveMatch bill, but she wasn't in dire straits.

"The things you're going to need are going to cost money," *Bubbe* said, lowering her voice. "You'll have to move out of that tiny, little apartment."

"I love my apartment," Lili said quietly. "*Bubbe,* if you're thinking about the wedding, don't worry. I don't need money for it."

Money to pay for the week of Hal's services, yes, Lili thought. *But for a wedding? Certainly not.*

"So he is going to marry you," *Bubbe* said in visible relief.

Lili had to force the lie. "He is my fiancé, *Bubbe.*"

"I just thought…well…" *Bubbe* flapped her hands and laughed. "I thought you were fighting because he wasn't going to the right thing by you."

That was uncomfortably close to what Lili had planned, and she was almost ready to agree. It would save a lot of headache if *Bubbe* already assumed Hal had broken off the engagement. They wouldn't have to go through the big fight scene tomorrow, after all. Before she could say anything, though, *Bubbe* laid the final brick in the wall.

"A man's not a real man if he won't stand by the mother of his child," *Bubbe* said.

"Child?" Lili said. "What are you talking about?"

"Eli told your mother all about what David said to you the other night. We know your little secret. It's okay, doll, really it is. It happens to lots of women." *Bubbe* leaned in again to share a secret. "Your own mother, *bubbeleh,* now she'll never tell you this—"

"Stop!" Lili cried, jumping to her feet . There was no way she wanted to hear any more of that little story. "You think I'm—"

"Pregnant!" *Bubbe* cried.

"Pregnant?" Lili shrieked.

"Pregnant?" Hal asked from the doorway. Then he turned and walked back out.

CHAPTER 9

Hal couldn't feel his feet. They were walking, carrying him down the hallway and out onto the front porch. But he couldn't feel them. Or, for that matter, his legs. Or his face. Or any part of his body.

Pregnant? But how could that be? They'd made love only just the night before, and he'd used protection. The child couldn't possibly be his.

He stopped before descending the stairs, his hand on the railing. Jealousy was foolish. Lili wasn't his. Her pregnancy wasn't any of his business. Hal took a few quick, deep breaths, forcing away the picture of a round-bellied Lili embracing a faceless man who was not him.

So she hadn't been completely honest about her reasons for hiring him. So what? The man in her life obviously wasn't going to be there for her, or she'd have brought him to meet her family instead of hapless Hal Kessler. She had hired him to do a job, and he'd done it. If she'd lied to him about why she needed him— Hal muttered a curse.

She'd lied. No matter how much he tried to convince himself it didn't matter, that she didn't matter, the fact remained Lili had lied to him. It hurt. He jumped down the stairs two at a time, almost willing himself to twist his ankle. Physical pain might take away the mental anguish.

"David!"

Lili had to call his name three more times before Hal realized she was calling him. He turned to see her hesitating at the top of the porch stairs. She took one step down, then stopped.

He thought about ignoring her and just walking on. Then he hung his head and went back to her. She met him at the bottom of the steps.

"It's not what you think," she began.

He held up his hand to silence her. "You don't owe me any explanations."

"Yes, I do." Lili let out a strangled laugh. "It's kinda funny actually."

Hal had never felt less like laughing. "I don't think I want to know."

He knew his reply was unyielding, and he ignored the small stab of nasty pleasure he got from seeing the surprise on her face. Lili licked her lips, and Hal was ashamed to see the sight could still move him. He didn't want to want her, but he did.

"If you'd let me explain," she said quietly.

When she reached for his hand, he didn't move to take hers. She let hers fall back to her side. Once more she let her tongue sweep the fullness of the lips he'd never taste again. She bit the soft flesh, gnawing nervously.

"It was a misunderstanding," she said when she saw he wasn't going to answer. "Something you told Eli."

"That's easy enough, isn't it?" Hal asked bitterly without waiting for her to finish. "Blame it on Hal. Hal's an easy scapegoat for everything. It's always Hal's fault."

"Please," she said miserably, and he was ashamed to see tears glittering in her eyes.

"You hired me for a job," he said in a low voice. "I believe I've done it. Your family thinks I'm some abusive cretin who beats you. They'll be more than thrilled when I'm gone. Isn't that what you wanted?"

"Yes, but—"

"I called a local cab company," Hal went on. The sight of her tears was enough to make him want to call back the words, to change his mind. But he pressed on. "They'll be here in forty minutes to take me to the bus station. I booked a ticket back to Harrisburg. I can be gone by this afternoon. And you can enjoy the rest of your vacation here with your family."

She shook her head. "You don't have to do that."

Hal glanced over her shoulder. Lili'd left the front door open, but the doorway wasn't empty. Eli and his wife Sarah stood framed in it. As Hal watched, they stepped through to be replaced by Ruth and Frank. One by one, the members of Lili's family came out onto the porch and stood by the railing to watch them.

Lili hadn't noticed their audience. She stepped toward him, reaching for his hand again. This time Hal jerked away. It was the perfect time for him to give Lili what she wanted. *To finish the job.*

"I think I have to," he said loudly. "What did you expect me to do, Lili?"

"I thought you'd let me tell you what happened," she said.

Hal made sure to keep his voice loud enough to carry to the army of relatives. "Right. Do you think any of your stupid explanations matter any more? I'm tired of listening to you and your worthless stories!"

Lili straightened her shoulders. "What?"

Hal grimaced, taking a step toward her that must have been menacing because she moved back. He jabbed his finger at her. "I'm tired of bowing and scraping for you, Lili! I'm sick of it! Staying with you has been the worst mistake I've ever made, and I intend to fix that right now!"

"Hal," she whispered. Her lower lip trembled. Tears spilled down her cheeks at last. "I'm sorry."

"Sorry's a bunch of crap, coming from you!" he cried.

He saw Eli move as though to come down the stairs, but Sarah held him back. At least Hal wouldn't have to get into a fistfight, too. He turned his attention back to Lili.

"You used me," he said. His voice broke over the words, and he realized he was no longer just acting for her family's benefit. "Lili, you never cared about me at all. You just used me for your own needs."

"That's not true," she said.

"Isn't it?" Hal threw out his hands and looked up at the sky. "Isn't that what our entire relationship has been about? You using me to get what you need? What you want? Hasn't this whole thing just been a huge lie?"

"No." She shook her head.

"No?" Hal let his hands fall to his sides. He felt exhausted. "Then tell me, Lili, what has it been, if not a complete and utter deception?"

She only looked at him helplessly. "I don't know."

What had he thought she might say? "Tell me you care about me, Lili."

She shook her head and began to back away. Hal did not follow her. His legs would not move. Somewhere he found the strength to call after her.

"Tell me you care about me!" he cried. "Tell me that last night wasn't just another lie!"

"I can't," she whispered brokenly. "Hal, please don't ask me to."

"All right," he said. "I understand."

"Please don't leave this way," Lili said so quietly he almost didn't hear her.

"What other way would you have me leave?" Hal asked her.

He didn't really expect a reply, and he didn't get one. Turning, Hal walked away. There wasn't anything else to say.

*   *   *

Lili watched Hal walk away, knowing she should run after him. She could tell him the truth, if only she knew what it was. Suddenly, the painful straightness of his gait and the way he walked was too much for her to bear. Lili turned to flee back into the main lodge.

They were watching her, nearly all of them. Her mother and siblings. *Bubbe* and *Zayde*. The aunts, the uncles, the cousins. Even the nieces and nephews stood clustered about their parents' legs, watching her humiliation.

Lili lifted her chin, determined not to break down in front of them. As her foot hit the bottom step, the irony of the situation struck her. This was what she'd planned all along. Hal had provided her with the perfect break up, complete with witnesses. Just one more thing she had him to thank for.

"Honey," her mom said as she reached the top of the stairs. Irene opened her arms wide, gathering Lili in.

The tears Lili had thought she might hold off fell hot and burning from her eyes. Something about her mother could always do that to her. She didn't fight the sobs, part of her knowing this was why she'd hired Hal, and another part unable to stop them even if she'd wanted.

Her mother hushed her and pulled her away from curious eyes. Lili was glad to be pulled for once; happy to have someone else in charge for a change. She didn't want to think about anything. She wanted to be a child again, when Mommy's kisses could make even the worst pain disappear.

"Now, Lilith, you sit down here and tell me everything," Irene ordered after she'd led Lili to the cozy front parlor.

Lili sank down into a chair close to the crackling fire. On either side of the fireplace, shelves crammed with books stretched from floor to ceiling. The room was small with a sliding pocket door to close it off from the front hallway. Lili caught a glimpse of the porch swing through the lace-curtained window. She turned her eyes away, not

100

wanting to think of the kisses she and Hal had shared on that swing.

"Oh, Mom." Lili sighed. Her hands plucked at the zipper on her jacket. "Where should I start?"

A small knock at the door kept her mother from replying right away. The door slid open and Ruth, Sarah and *Bubbe* came through. *Bubbe* and Lili's mom shared another of their unfathomable looks, but Ruth just looked mad. She strode immediately to Lili's side and drew her sister into a fierce embrace.

"That bastard!" She said. "Frank and Eli are ready to hunt him down for you, Lili, if you want them to."

The thought of her brother and brother-in-law going after Hal made Lili push her sister away. "No, Ruthie. This is my problem."

Sarah slipped into chair across from Lili's. "What can we do for you?"

Lili looked around at the women who wanted to protect her as they all found seats in the small parlor. They'd only ever acted out of concern for her. Again, waves of guilt rocked her. She took a deep breath, deciding it was time to come clean.

"Hal is not my fiancé," she said.

"Hal who?" Ruth asked.

"I mean David." Lili took another deep breath. This was going to be hard. "His name is really Hal."

"So then why do you call him David?" Ruth asked.

"Lili Alster," her mother said. "I think you've got some real explaining to do."

"I hired him from an escort service," Lili explained.

"Why on earth would you do that?" Sarah asked.

Lili rubbed her eyes. "I had been telling you all along that I'd finally found a new man. When you started insisting I bring him along this week, I had to find somebody. Hiring someone was my only option."

"Not your only option, young lady," *Bubbe* sniffed. "You could've just told us the truth."

Lili met each of their eyes in turn. "I didn't want to disappoint you. You all were so excited that I'd finally started dating again."

"Of course we were excited," Ruth said. "We just wanted to see you happy—"

"I know," Lili interrupted. "The problem was, none of you would see that I was happy. Am happy. With the way my life is."

"Lili, you can't keep mourning Ian forever," Irene said quietly. "He was a good man, and we know you loved him, but—"

A short, harsh bark of laughter shot out of Lili's mouth. "Oh, Mom. This is where it all began. With Ian."

"What about Ian?" Ruth asked.

Lili again picked at her zipper, preferring to look at her hands rather than her family. "It's my fault Ian died."

"*Bubbeleh,* I thought we were through with that," her grandmother said. "Wet roads and careless driving caused the accident. You couldn't have stopped it."

Now was the time to unburden herself of the secret she'd kept for so long. Lili felt a sense of sick relief, frightened to at last tell her family the truth about Ian and overjoyed to release herself from the past.

"Ian wouldn't have been on the road that night, driving so fast, if he and I hadn't fought." She swallowed hard, trying to find the right words. "I—we—I broke up with Ian that night. I told him I didn't want to marry him. He was angry and upset. He threatened me."

"Threatened you?" Ruth gasped. "No!"

Now Lili forced herself to meet her sister's gaze squarely. "Ian often threatened me, Ruth. He was very controlling. He wanted to determine my every move, from the perfume I wore to the way I ordered my steak."

She could see they were having trouble reconciling their memories of the perfect fiancé with this new picture Lili was painting. Ruth still looked angry, but now she also looked confused. Gentle Sarah only looked sorry. *Bubbe* and Lili's mom shook their heads as though unable to comprehend the story Lili was telling.

"He told me that, after we were married, I was going to have to quit my job because no wife of his was going work."

"Lili, you love your job!" Sarah exclaimed.

"I usually gave in to his demands, but this time I said no." Lili shivered, remembering the way Ian's handsome face had turned dark with fury. "I told him I was tired of him trying to change me, and that I would decide whether or not I'd quit. Not him." She paused, not wanting to admit what came next but knowing she would have to. "Then he hit me."

"No!" Cried her mother in horror.

"*Oy, oy, oy,*" moaned *Bubbe,* throwing her hands up to cover her mouth.

"He didn't," Ruth said flatly. "Oh, Lili, why didn't you tell us?"

"The bruises were easy to explain away," Lili said. "And he was dead. You all thought he was so wonderful. I didn't think telling you the truth would help."

"It would've helped *you*," Sarah told her. "Lili, you could have told us."

"So all this time you haven't been mourning him at all?" Ruth questioned. "Then why have you been keeping to yourself?"

"I didn't ever want to give so much of myself away again," Lili said firmly. "For a while you all left me alone because you thought I needed time to get over Ian. It was a good excuse. But then you kept bugging me."

"We drove you into a corner," Ruth said ruefully, sitting back in her chair. "Lili, if I'd known, I never would've kept asking you."

"I would have," *Bubbe* said snappily. "Makes no sense, a pretty girl like you, hiding herself away like that."

Lili smiled at her grandmother. "You wanted so much for me to find someone new, to settle down. I thought if I told you I'd found somebody, we could break up and then I'd buy myself some more time."

"She's too smart," *Bubbe* said grudgingly to Irene.

Lili's mom sighed. "So you hired David? Hal? Whatever his name is?"

Lili nodded. "I told him to be a real jerk, so you'd all be happy when we broke up."

"I can't say I approve of all this," her mother said. "Lies are never the right choice."

"They always come back to haunt you in the end," Lili finished one of her mother's favorite sayings. "I know, Ma. And I'm sorry."

"So he's not a doctor?" *Bubbe* asked.

Her grandmother sounded so disappointed, Lili nearly laughed. "No, *Bubbe*. Hal's in school to become a massage therapist. And even though he is a little clumsy, he's not the jerk you all think he is."

"I don't understand," *Bubbe* said. "So if you two aren't engaged, how'd you end up pregnant?"

Lili hung her head, at a loss to explain. "I'm not pregnant."

"But David, I mean Hal, told Eli you were knocked up!" Sarah said.

Lili frowned. All at once she remembered the night at dinner with Hal's socially inept responses. "I don't think he meant it that way. Anyhow, I'm not pregnant."

"*Oy,* that's a relief," *Bubbe* said. "So, when's he coming back?"

"He's not coming back, *Bubbe,*" Lili said. "He's gone."

"I thought the break up was just fake," *Bubbe* insisted.

"It was. But it was real." Lili shrugged. "It's hard to explain."

Bubbe chuckled. "Doll, you're telling me."

There was no way Lili was going to admit to her mother and grandmother that she'd gone to bed with Hal. "Hal's a good guy. He didn't deserve to get tangled up in all of this. It's better that he left."

"But you're going to see him again, right?" *Bubbe* persisted.

"No, *Bubbe*," Lili said as patiently as she could. "I told you, Hal and I weren't really dating. I hired him from an escort agency."

"Escort, shmescort," *Bubbe* said. "Maybe that's how it started, *bubbeleh,* but you can't tell me that's how it ended up."

Lili's cheeks burned. "Of course it is. Hal did what I hired him to do, and now he's on his way back to Pennsylvania. I'll send the check to the agency next week and that's the end of it."

"That's not the end," *Bubbe* said firmly with a wag of her finger. "You're too crazy about that man, Lilith Alster."

"Hal's a nice guy," Lili said stiffly, not wanting the conversation to go any further. "But there's nothing between us—"

"And he's bonkers about you, doll," *Bubbe* cut in. "It was all over his face. I never saw a man more enthralled with a gal than him over you."

"You're wrong," Lili said, feeling the tears threaten her again.

"No?" *Bubbe* asked. "How can you be so sure?"

Because of the way I treated him, Lili thought. Because she'd used him and hurt him, and even if there had been some feelings between them, they'd certainly been destroyed now. Hal had done his job, and that was all.

"I'm sure," Lili whispered.

"You wait and see," *Bubbe* said with a pat to Lili's hand. "You give him a second chance."

Lili wished she could believe her grandmother. Then she remembered the look on Hal's face just before he'd walked away. There would be no second chances. And why should there be? After the way she'd treated him, she didn't deserve any.

* * *

Hal didn't feel like fighting the sweet, old lady with the knitting bag for the window seat. Despite her kindly smile, she looked as though she could be nasty with her needles. Hal slid into the aisle seat with a resigned sigh, though the window seat had been his first choice.

"Rule number one," the old lady advised him as he sat. "Never go to the bathroom on a bus."

Hal looked at her. "What's rule number two?"

She shook her needles at him. "Don't eat at the taco stand when we make the rest stop. Otherwise you'll have to break rule number one. Frequently."

She chuckled loudly at her own joke, slapping her leg with the hand not holding the lethal looking needles. "Oh, I crack myself up."

Hal didn't feel like smiling. He just nodded and stretched his legs as much as he could, easing the seat back from its uncomfortable position to one only marginally more restful. He thought he might sleep. Night had fallen and the bus was dark.

Until, that was, the old lady who'd stolen his seat turned on her light. "Musta dropped a stitch," she muttered, fingering the pile of pink yarn in her lap. "Dang. Why's that always happen?"

She shoved the straggly mess toward Hal. "Here. Can you see if there's a hole in there anywhere?"

Hal squinted half-heartedly at the mess and shook his head. "No. Sorry."

"Huh." His seatmate grunted. "Dang."

She turned off the light. Hal closed his eyes and tried to sleep. His mind whirled with thoughts of Lili.

The lady turned on the light again. "Sonny, c'mon. Help an old lady out. If I don't get this stitched up right my Poochie's gonna be wearing a sweater with only three legs."

Gritting his teeth, Hal snatched the sorry looking pile of pink yarn and squeezed it. "There. Is that what you're looking for?"

"That's it, all right." The old lady nodded vigorously and began unraveling her creation. "Perfect."

Hal leaned back again. The clack-clacking of the needles next to him was soothing. Despite the annoying overhead light, he began to drift.

"What's her name anyway?" his seatmate asked abruptly.

Hal's eyes flew open and he sat up. The old lady kept clacking contentedly. "What?"

"The name of the lady who done made your face turn so sour." She peeked over at him with a wry grin on her wrinkled face. "There is one, ain't there? A lady?"

"I'm trying to sleep," Hal said unkindly.

"Sure, sure," said the old lady without offense. "Just thought you might like to talk about it, that's all."

Hal settled further into his uncomfortable seat. Another four hours on this bus seemed unbearable. Maybe he'd get lucky and they'd hit some sort of freaky time warp or something.

Time Warp. Lili. He thought of her singing that ridiculous song, and he groaned.

"C'mon, sonny," prompted the old lady. "Tell me all about her. She's pretty, I'll bet."

"Yes," Hal said reluctantly. "Very pretty."

"But you walked away from her." The clacking paused, and she reached down to the bag between her feet and pulled out a skein of orange yarn. Her needles flashed as she started knitting again.

"It was what she wanted," Hal said.

"But not what you wanted?" She looked at him shrewdly. "You couldn't change her mind?"

"It's not that simple," Hal said. He thought of trying to explain the situation and found he couldn't.

"Ain't much in this world that is, sonny." The lady chuckled again, knitting furiously. "Ain't much that is."

Hal finally fell to sleep with the sound of her needles clacking in his mind. He didn't dream, or if he did, they were bland and forgettable. When he woke, it was in the Harrisburg station.

"Don't look so down, sonny," his seatmate advised him as he helped her off the bus. "Thing's always work out for the best."

The best would be if Lili had told him what he wanted to hear. *Since I don't have that,* Hal thought, *I'll just have to hope something else comes along.*

The morning sun was just beginning to break when he finally got home. The cab driver offered to help him wrangle the overstuffed suitcase up the stairs to his apartment building, but Hal didn't have enough money to tip the guy any more. He said he'd do it himself.

"Take care, buddy," the driver said with a tip of his hat. "Get some sleep. You look like you need it."

As much he might seek to avoid thinking of Lili in the solace of sleep, he wasn't tired. He set about unpacking his case by tossing the entire contents onto his bed. Of everything he'd packed, he'd used only a few things.

"So much for being prepared," he said to the empty room.

His voice practically echoed, and for the first time, Hal took the time to really look around. He'd lived in this apartment for a year now. The walls were still bare and dingy white, without so much as a cheap, framed print to brighten them. The furniture, what little he had, was a jumbled mix of Salvation Army bargains and expensive items he'd managed to salvage from his divorce. His bed was nothing more than a bare mattress and box spring laid on the floor, his linens mismatched and ugly.

Hal sat on his pitiful excuse for a bed and rested his head in his hands. He didn't miss the fancy house, the car, the luxury vacations. Truthfully, he didn't even miss Cassie. *But living like this is just damn depressing.*

His gaze fell on the dented metal filing cabinet he was using as a nightstand. He had paperwork to fill out for LoveMatch. He pulled out the forms and began checking off the necessary boxes. When he got to the section titled "extraordinary circumstances," he stopped. Falling in love could be considered extraordinary. His pen hovered above the stark lines, so black against the unforgiving whiteness of the paper. Then he wrote "none."

CHAPTER 10

"I'm sorry, dear." Muriel Whitehead's nasal voice sounded sympathetic. "But Hal left LoveMatch three weeks ago."

Three weeks ago. That meant he'd quit immediately after returning from New York. Lili felt incredibly stupid for even having called. "Oh, I didn't know. Can you give me his home phone number?"

A long silence met her request, and Lili knew the answer was going to be no. Ms. Whitehead sighed heavily into the phone. "It's against LoveMatch policy. It's to protect our escorts."

"I understand," Lili said. "So giving me his address is out, too."

"I'm sorry, honey," Ms. Whitehead said. She really did sound sorry, too, but that wasn't going to help Lili find him.

"Can you at least tell me his last name?"

She could practically hear the woman squirming on the other end. "We sign confidentiality agreements for all our escorts," Ms. Whitehead said. "I'm sorry."

"Okay. Thanks anyway." *For nothing,* Lili thought.

"No problem, honey. And if you ever need another escort—"

"Thanks, but I don't think I will." Lili hung up the phone and sat back in her chair.

Rain pattered against her windowpane and she'd turned on the gas fireplace. Soft music played from the stereo. She'd poured a glass of wine. The mood was romantic, except for one thing. She was alone.

Lili went to the kitchen and dumped her wine down the drain. She flicked the stereo off with one finger, leaving only the sound of the rain to serenade her as she curled up in front of the fire again. The curling, writhing flames mesmerized her.

For three weeks she'd fought against thinking of Hal. She'd paid the bill when it came from the agency, wincing at the amount. The trip had cost her more than just the amount she wrote on the check. She didn't want to think about how much.

Her family, for once, was keeping their distance. Even *Bubbe* didn't ask about Lili's love life during her weekly phone calls. For Lili, the unaccustomed restraint only made the problem worse. Instead of helping her forget Hal , the obvious way they ignored the subject meant she couldn't stop thinking about him.

When she found herself in the convenience store clutching a package of hand warmers and biting her lip to keep from crying and laughing at the same time, Lili knew she could no longer ignore her feelings. She wanted—needed—to talk to Hal. She had no real hope that things between them might be resolved, but she had to try.

It was easy to make the decision, but hard to work up the courage to follow through. After reaching the LoveMatch voice mail this evening, she'd almost backed out. But the message clearly stated to contact Muriel Whitehead in case of emergency, and so Lili called the woman at home.

Not that she'd been any help, Lili thought sourly. *Confidentiality agreements! For the escort's protection?* She grudgingly admitted the possibility of a client taking a date too far, pursuing her escort off duty and becoming a menace. Still, the policy had really thrown a monkey wrench in her plans.

"She could've at least told me his last name," Lili said aloud, grumbling. Her legs were stiffening, and she stretched them out, wishing for a massage. That thought reminded her all too clearly of Hal's massage, and the lovemaking which had followed.

"Damn!" she cursed, pounding her thigh. She had to find him. If for no other reason than to tell him the truth. Yes, she had hired him to serve her purpose, but everything else had come from her heart.

Suddenly an idea sprang fully formed into her mind. It was so ludicrous, so insane, that it just might work. Grinning wildly, Lili picked up the phone.

"Ms. Whitehead?" she said, barely suppressing a crazy chuckle. "I've changed my mind. I need an escort after all."

*   *   *

"Yo, Kessler!" It was Rick, Hal's former LoveMatch co-worker.

"Rick," Hal said without enthusiasm. "How's it going?"

"They're hanging low, buddy." Rick guffawed, reaching over the bar to slap Hal on the arm. "We miss you around the stud barn."

"Sure," Hal said, unconvinced. "What'll you have?"

Rick named an import beer and tossed a handful of pretzels in his mouth. "How long you been working here?"

Hal topped off the glass and pushed it across to Rick. "About two-and-a-half weeks."

"Sweet." Rick surveyed the bar and tossed back half his beer. "Classy place."

Hal managed not to roll his eyes. The place was hardly upscale.

"You on a date?" Hal asked, praying Rick's answer would be yes. That meant he wouldn't have to suffer the other man's presence very long.

"Oh, yeah, man." Rick waggled his eyebrows. "We're going here for drinks, then to some charity function."

"Sounds nice," Hal said noncommittally. He looked down the bar, hoping for another customer so he could leave Rick. The place was dead, though.

"So what's up with you anyway?" Rick asked, suddenly serious. "Why'd you leave the biz?"

Surprised by Rick's interest, Hal thought about his reply. "I got tired of it."

The brief moment of intellect faded with Rick's reply. "Man, are you an idiot. Give up all the dough and the parties? And the action? They'll have to drag me away from this job."

Hal shrugged, wiping the bar with a damp cloth. "Not me."

"Ah, man." Rick downed the last of his beer, then wiped the foam from his lip with the back of his hand. "You let one of 'em get to you, huh?"

"What?" Hal stopped wiping, stunned at Rick's unexpected insight.

Rick shook his head, frowning. "Dude, you can't do that. You—you—" He gestured in the air as though wanting to form a thought, but not quite able to. "They're just women, Hal. You can't let them get inside you, man. Sure, they tell you you're the best lover they've ever had. They buy you expensive stuff. They take you to great places and tell you how great you are. But it's not real, man."

Rick sighed heavily, voice filled with a depth of emotion of which Hal would have thought him incapable. "Man, these babes will mess you up." He looked around circumspectly. "You know the worst ones?

The ugly ones, dude. They're so glad to be seen with you, they tell you all this nice stuff, get you thinking you're something special, but when it comes down to it, man—they only want you for one thing. Your body."

Hal might have laughed if Rick wasn't being so obviously truthful. "Sorry to hear that... dude."

"Dude." Rick nodded. Hal poured him another beer and Rick drank that. The men sat in silence for a moment, contemplating women and their fickle natures.

"That what happened to you?"

There'd been no expensive gifts. Lili hadn't told him how great he was, or that he was the best lover. He'd let her inside him, though, hadn't he? Let her crawl right in there and, as Rick so aptly put it, mess him up?

"Yeah," Hal said. "Hell, yes. That's what happened to me."

*   *   *

"And that's where I learned to mambo." Lili's escort smiled suavely and ran his fingers through his dark, slick hair. "Care to try?"

"Uh, no." Lili smiled. "No, thanks, Derek."

Derek shrugged lightly. "It's your night."

Lili stifled a groan. It sure was. From the cocktails to the appetizers and then to dinner, not to mention the LoveMatch fee. It was all hers. Right out of her checkbook and into the LoveMatch coffers.

Derek was her third LoveMatch date in two weeks. He was a handsome man. Well, they all were. He was well-groomed and attentive. Even, Lili admitted, well-spoken. His manners were near perfection, and he listened to her as though he actually cared about what she had to say. If she wasn't paying an arm and a leg to have him sit across from her, Lili might have been flattered.

"Derek, do you like what you do?" she asked as the waiter brought their desserts.

He seemed taken aback by her question. "I certainly do."

"Why?"

He gave her the same answer Hal had, only his came with a smarmy grin that completely turned Lili off. "I like to spend my time in the company of attractive ladies like yourself."

"Have you been working for LoveMatch a long time?"

Now he seemed disconcerted. "Lili, is this really what you want to talk about?"

"Yes," she said firmly, heading for some specific information, but knowing she couldn't just come right out and ask. "Do you have a problem with it?"

Derek forked a bite of chocolate cream pie into his mouth and chewed slowly, then swallowed. "No. But usually my ladies like to talk about themselves."

"I'm really interested," Lili said.

"I've been an escort for three years," Derek said finally.

So he'd have known Hal. "Is there a lot of turnover in the company?"

If he found her questions strange, he was well-trained enough not to show it. "Sure. We get a lot of guys through who just need money for a while. Or they think it's going to be some great sex gig—" Derek paused and looked embarrassed. "Sorry. We're not supposed to talk about that."

"I won't tell," Lili promised. "Do you guys ever hang out when you're not working?"

Now Derek looked a little scared. "Why do you ask?"

"Just curious." Lili bit her own chocolate pie, which was like sawdust in her mouth. It would be so much easier if she could just come right out and ask him if he knew Hal, but she'd learned the hard way from date number one that the LoveMatch confidentiality agreement was incredibly revered. None of the escorts wanted to be tracked down by desperate, lovesick clients.

"We hang out at the gym sometimes." Derek pushed his pie away, as though he no longer could stomach it. "Yeah, sometimes we get together for drinks. Watch the game. Stuff like that."

Now she was getting somewhere. "Anybody you particularly like to hang out with?"

Derek's gaze grew wary. He lowered his voice to a whisper. "Who sent you?"

"What?" Lili had no idea what he could mean.

Derek's fingers clutched at his napkin. "Did Brandon send you?"

"Who?" All of a sudden Lili felt like she'd stepped into a big pile of something warm. And not chocolate pie.

"He did, didn't he?" Derek sat back, jaw clenched. "I told him it's just a job!"

"Whoa, wait a minute." Lili was getting the picture, and it was one she didn't particularly want in her mental photo album. "You and Brandon are—"

"He's my boyfriend," Derek said, as though she should know. "You mean he didn't send you to spy on me?"

Lili shook her head. Now Derek looked chastened and a little scared. His fingers folded the cloth napkin nervously.

"It's okay," Lili said. She had an idea that Derek's regular clientele might not be too thrilled to learn what she just had. "Brandon didn't send me. I'm just trying to get some information about one of your former co-workers."

Derek looked so relieved, Lili thought he might kiss her. "Why didn't you just ask?"

"Confidentiality," Lili whispered.

Derek leaned across the table and Lili caught the scent of his cologne. Something spicy and insolent. Sexy. He flashed her a look with his dark eyes and smiled a slow, sensuous grin that she knew was contrived. She felt it ripple through her anyway.

"I'll keep yours if you keep mine," he said.

"His name is Hal," Lili said. "And I want to find him."

*   *   *

"I'll have another one of these." The attractive blonde sitting at the bar tilted her head toward her drink. She plucked the sodden paper umbrella out of it and twirled it between her fingers. "Please."

"Coming right up." The night was young, but Hal was already exhausted. Last night had been dead in here, but tonight's crowd came seeking hot wings and cold drinks at Thursday night prices. Though he normally shared the bar with another 'tender, the other guy had called off. Hal had to work the crowd alone. That, on top of a heavy day of classes and little sleep for the past few weeks—he wasn't exactly feeling like Tom Cruise in the movie where he flung the bottles around.

"Hal, you got those wings ready yet?" Sandy, the waitress, stepped behind the bar to grab a couple of beers.

Hal glanced over his shoulder to check the counter next to the kitchen doors. "Not out yet, Sandy. Sorry."

"Shoot." Sandy blew a strand of dark brown hair out of her eyes. "They're gonna start screaming for blood instead of blue cheese."

"Another drink?" the blonde asked impatiently, wiggling her paper umbrella at Hal.

He nodded, pushed past Sandy and headed for the blender. "Right away."

"Hey, buddy, can I get another couple of shots over here?"

"Waiting on daiquiri!"

"How about a rum and Coke?"

Where are they all coming from? Hal felt like he was being attacked by a bunch of zombies, only ones that weren't hungry for flesh. This crowd of creeping undead wanted booze.

He poured drinks, passed platters of wings and generally tried to keep from being bowled over by the crowd. Hal wouldn't have said he was enjoying himself, but there was a sense of relief in the brain-numbing repetition of the tasks before him. It gave his mind a rest from the constant cycle of thoughts about Lili.

Everything was going along like a well-orchestrated waltz. It wasn't until Sandy came back behind the bar again that Hal remembered he was a terrible dancer.

The beer went flying, aided by the hot wings. Hal crunched broken glass and blue cheese under foot while Sandy yelped. The bar groaned collectively.

"I'll get the mop," Sandy said. She patted him on the arm. "Don't worry about it, Hal."

Wearily, Hal began sweeping up glass and gunk. The restless, booze-craving zombies shuffled impatiently at the bar, muttering amongst themselves. *What perfect metaphor for my life,* Hal thought with more than a little bitterness. *Shattered heart and gunked-up emotions.* If he could sweep away the five days he'd spent with Lili as easily as he swept away the broken glass, he'd be set.

"Hal, buddy!"

The familiar voice automatically set Hal's jaw even as he turned. Rick had muscled his way up to the bar, seeming not to notice the nasty glares he got from the other customers. He rapped the bar top with his knuckles.

"Dude, grab me a beer, will ya?"

Hal held up the broom. "I'm a little busy here, Rick."

It took Rick a moment to look around and see he wasn't the only person in the room. A long, painful moment. "Oh, sure, man. Yeah. Whatever. I'll wait for it."

Shaking his head, Hal finished clearing the floor of the worst of the mess, then set about filling all the drink orders. Surprisingly, once he'd found his rhythm again, clearing away the backlogged crowd didn't take very long. *Or maybe they were afraid I'll drop a plateful of wings on them,* Hal thought.

Once the free Happy Hour snack buffet opened up, the undead moved away from the bar to scarf down cheese sticks, onion rings, and a plethora of other fried bar fare. Hal actually found himself with a moment to breathe. Sandy took the opportunity for a smoke break. Rick sat at the bar and drank his beer.

"I'm on another date." Rick spoke up when it became clear Hal had a free minute.

Hal, who'd been hoping for the chance to grab a sandwich from the kitchen, managed a smile. "You're on a roll. Uh, dude."

"Dude!" It seemed Rick could make just that one word mean any number of things, just by using a different tone of voice. This time it clearly meant he was happy. "And man, this babe is sweet!"

"Yeah?" Hal asked, not really caring. His stomach grumbled, especially when he looked out and saw the zombies chowing down like the world was about to end. When Sandy got back, he'd get something to eat.

Rick made a waving motion with his hand and jerked his head back and forth. "Oh, yeah. Dude, she is a hottie! And I think she really digs me."

"Good for you," Hal said, keeping his eye out for Sandy's return. "Dude."

"Dude!" Rick replied with a sly grin. "She made an emergency request for me, man. Whitehead cancelled my other gig 'cause this babe was so hot for me."

"Cool," Hal said. Finally, he spotted Sandy weaving her way through the crowd back to the bar.

"I'm getting laid for sure tonight," Rick said. "And I won't even have to fake it with this babe. Let me tell you, man, she is hot!"

"You said that," Hal told him. Rick's rambling was becoming more than just background noise. It was starting to get on his nerves. "Hey, Sandy!"

"I thought she might want to go to Wanda's Beach Club or someplace." Rick shrugged. "But she insisted we come here. Whatever. Dude, one place to get beer's as good as any, am I right?"

"Especially when you're not paying for it," Hal said absently. Sandy had gotten hung up in a gaggle of mini-skirted singletons who appeared to be asking her if their hair looked all right.

"Dude, you are so right." Rick drained the last of his beer and Hal handed him another.

"So where is this mystery woman?" Hal asked, not that he cared. It looked like Sandy was going to be a few more minutes.

"She had to hit the ladies'. Freshen herself up for me, you know." Rick let out a lusty chuckle that made Hal grimace. "Dude!"

"Dude," Hal agreed. His stomach protested its chronic emptiness again, and he decided he couldn't wait any longer. "I'll be right back, all right? If anyone comes up, just tell them to wait a second."

"Sure, man." Rick happily went back to sucking down his draft.

Hal put in a quick order for a roast beef sandwich and fries, then ducked back to the bar. The crowd still hovered around the buffet, though the contents of most of the warming trays had been demolished. Rick's date had finally made it back from the bathroom.

They'd moved to the far end of the bar. Rick had his arm around the lady fair who was perusing the crowd. From the back, she looked slim with sleek dark hair that reminded him disconcertingly of Lili's. When she turned around, Hal saw why. The woman with Rick was Lili.

No. It couldn't be. *Lili with Rick, of all people?* Why had she hired another LoveMatch escort? The sight of her with another man, another paid man, hit him like a punch to the gut.

Hal took a step back, forgetting he had no place to go. Sandy finally managed to work her way through back to him, and now she chirped perkily, "If you need a break or something—"

"I'll take it," Hal said.

He stepped out from behind the bar, heading for the door, just as Lili turned and saw him.

"Hal!" she cried, but he ignored her.

He pushed through the crowd, slammed through the doors, and was gone.

*   *   *

"Babe, you know Kessler?" Rick asked her, holding her by the arm as Lili tried to go after Hal.

"Yes," Lili said impatiently, shaking him off. "That's why I wanted to come here. Because you knew him."

"Huh?"

She didn't have time to explain to Rick, who was easy on the eyes but incredibly difficult on the intellect. "Listen, Rick, I've got to go."

"But—wait!" Rick called after her. Lili didn't turn, even when she heard him cry forlornly, "Dude?"

The crowd seemed determined to keep her from getting out. She dodged one couple grappling in the first stages of drunken courtship, then had to squeeze between a group of women huddled together around a high table. Determined she would catch up to Hal if it meant driving her heel into some poor slob's instep, Lili pushed her way through the throng.

"Hal!" she cried to the night, but he was gone.

She searched the street from side to side, and didn't see him. Her heart hit the pavement, followed by her stomach, but then she looked again. She saw just a flash of his yellow shirt as he turned the corner into an alley only two blocks ahead.

She didn't bother calling out again, needing to save her breath for the jog ahead. Grateful she'd gone with the sensible low-heeled boots instead of the sexy slingback pumps she'd first picked out, Lili took off at a run. Freezing air made the inside of her nose and lungs burn as she ran, but that didn't stop her.

She splashed through a puddle of icy water, squeaking when it hit her stocking covered calves. And still she ran on. One block more. She had to turn the corner before he turned again. Before she lost him again.

Just ahead, the street lamp flickered obnoxiously, casting the alley Hal had gone down into deep shadow. Now Lili hesitated. Did she really want to run down a dark alley at night, wearing an outfit chosen especially to entice a man?

She looked down the street in both directions, but other than an occasional flash of headlights from the next corner, it was deserted. Light and music spilled out of Zane's just two blocks down, but here the storefronts were dark and locked up for the night.

I lost him once, Lili thought. She wouldn't do it again. Heart pounding, she dove into the alley and prepared to run after the man who'd gotten away with her heart.

Before her eyes could adjust to the even darker alley, Lili ran head first into a brick wall. At least, it felt like a brick wall, albeit one wearing a yellow shirt. Both of them went down hard, rolling into a pile of cardboard and garbage overflowing from a dumpster.

Her knees stung and her stockings were shredded ruins. Hal's elbow had caught her painfully just beneath the ribs, and her breath came in labored, whistling gasps. She had never been so happy in her life.

"Hal!"

Hal wheezed. Lili felt him move beneath her, his hands pushing feebly at her knee. It had lodged between his legs. High up between his legs.

The garbage, piled precariously as it was, shifted and slid. Hal and Lili rolled to the cold, wet pavement. She didn't want to think about what was squelching beneath him.

"I know what you must be thinking," she began. "About why I was with Rick."

"It's not a story I need to hear right now," Hal replied, his voice still harsh with pain. "Not in a pile of garbage."

"When you ran out, I thought I'd blown it again," Lili admitted.

Hal shook his head. "Lili, I was coming back to talk to you. I decided I'd run out on you once, and I wasn't going to do it again."

She didn't want to move, but the pavement was cold and the garbage none too fragrant. "Hal—"

But he interrupted her. "This is how we first met. Maybe…maybe we can start again. I'm Hal Kessler."

"I'm Lili Alster," Lili said. "And I'm pleased to meet you."

They needed no more introduction than that because then he pulled her mouth to his for a kiss made even sweeter for how long she'd thought about having it.

Life with Hal will mean a lot of falling, Lili thought as together they hobbled to the streetlamp's glow.

Falling in love.

MEGAN HART

Megan Hart began her writing career in grammar school when she plagiarized a short story by Ray Bradbury. She soon realized that making up her own stories was better than copying other people's, and she's been writing ever since.

Megan's award-winning short fiction has appeared in such diverse publications as *Hustler*, *On Our Backs* and *The Reaper*. Her novels include every genre of romance, from historical to steamy futuristic SF. In addition to her short erotic fiction for the Amber Kisses imprint, look for her other Amber Quill novels: *Riverboat Bride, Lonesome Bride, Convicted!* and *Love Match.*

Megan's current projects include a fantasy series, a futuristic trilogy and a dramatic suspense novel. Her dream is to have a movie made of every one of her novels, starring herself as the heroine and Keanu Reeves as the hero. Megan lives in the deep, dark woods of Pennsylvania with her husband and two monsters...er...children.

Learn more about Megan by visiting her website:
http://www.meganhart.com

*   *   *

Don't miss Pot Of Gold, by Megan Hart, available Winter, 2004
from Amber Quill Press, LLC

When Eleanor Fitzwilliam stows away on her fiancé's ship, The Rainbow, *the last thing in the world she expects to find on deck is another man...and a pirate, at that! Captain Robin Steele claims he stole a magic coin from a drunken leprechaun on holiday in the Caribbean. Now all he has to do is follow the coin and he'll find the leprechaun's fabled pot of gold. But when Eleanor steals the coin and demands he split the money with her, they both discover a treasure of another sort...Love.*